# RUNNING
## TO
# GRACELAND

# RUNNING
## TO
# GRACELAND

**A NOVEL**

69 PRO 160

**JOHN SLAYTON**

ISBN 13: 978-1-63489-111-0
eISBN: 978-1-63489-112-7

Library of Congress Catalog Number: 2018930310
Printed in the United States of America
First Printing: 2018

22  21  20  19  18          5  4  3  2  1

Cover and interior design by Dan Pitts.

Wise Ink Creative Publishing
837 Glenwood Avenue
www.wiseinkpub.com

*To Bambo*

"All I wanted was to go somewheres; all I wanted was a change."

— Huckleberry Finn

# Mile Marker Less Than 0

## (July 1981)

Curtis's Dodge Dart roared over the rough asphalt as we sped north on Highway 41. Curtis had the accelerator jammed to the floorboard, and the car was edging faster. I rode shotgun, air blasting my face.

"Come on, man." Bruce leaned forward from the back seat and peeked his head between us. "Ease up. It's not like anything's chasing us."

Curtis wrung his hands on the steering wheel. He held it so tight that even in the dim light of the dashboard the scars on his knuckles burned ghost white. He got those scars a couple of months back after a fight with his dad when he punched their concrete-block house. Not a good idea. His dad was dead a month later. He had a bad heart.

Curtis turned and shot Bruce a look, that half smile of his like he was in on some joke that you just wouldn't get. And when Curtis started to get that look, there was nothing you could say to him. All you could do was hang on and hope you made it safe to the other side. He was getting like that more and more lately, ever since he got out. He was really intense that night. Maybe because this was likely the last time the three of us would take off like this. Bruce was headed to Gainesville in a couple of weeks. God knows where Curtis and I were headed. The future loomed before us like a brick wall, and we were in a rocket ship screaming right at it.

The front end trembled as the speedometer needle wobbled toward a hundred. My heart started to pump hard, juiced by the swelling rattle of the car. Afraid to turn away, I scanned the rush of asphalt racing through the field of light ahead. And Curtis. Man, that look. I didn't know how far he was going to take it this time. My fingers dug into the armrest, holding on. Like that would do any good if we started cartwheeling down the side of the highway. I was glad his Dart couldn't do much more than a hundred.

"Come on, man," Bruce pleaded.

Curtis ignored him. He leaned forward and looked up through the windshield. "You know, when I was little—"

"Keep your eyes on the damn road!" Bruce yelled.

"—I used to think that was where all the dead people went. That it was like where heaven was."

I followed his gaze. The moon hung high above the silhouette of the forest ahead, glowing and big, like the X-ray of a smeared thumbprint. "The moon?"

"Yeah." A back tire ground against the shoulder of the road. "Shit!" Curtis snapped his eyes down. He cut the wheel and pressed down on the brake. The tires barked, and the Dart veered across the road into the left lane. Curtis pulled it back over with a chirp. He laughed, then slammed the accelerator back to the floor.

"Damn, Curtis! Keep your fucking eyes on the road." Bruce said. "How much farther is it, anyway?"

"Almost there."

Curtis's uncle owned a hunting cabin in the Ocala National Forest. He had told Curtis that he could use the place whenever he wanted. That's what Curtis said, anyway, and all it took for us to throw our sleeping bags and camping gear in the trunk and take off.

It seemed we were doing something like that every weekend. Taking off for somewhere. And these days, it seemed that Curtis wanted to take it further and further. These days he was out of control. Part of me didn't blame him. Life can deal you a shit sandwich, and his had dried cow chips on top. But I know I sure as hell wanted to get somewhere, to find something. I don't know. Mostly, I guess we were trying to get away from the shitty lives we had. It can eat at you after a while, make you restless as hell. Maybe it's the other way around. Maybe it was that restlessness that twisted us up and made us want to go some place, to find something, even though we had no idea what the hell we were looking for.

I sucked down the last foamy swallow from my Busch tall boy, all the while peering around the can, not wanting to take my eyes off the road for a second. I threw the empty out the window and reached back. Bruce slapped a fresh one into my grasp. I'd need a few more before this ride was over.

Curtis took a slug off his beer. "I read an article in *Outdoor Life* about fishing in Canada. My dad used to go fishing in British Columbia. He said it was great. Letting your beer get cold in the river. Frying up a trout over a fire at the end of the day. That's the life, man. Think about it. Free from all the bullshit. You want to do it, Jack. Take off now and never come back."

He looked to me. For a second, I did want to, and, for a second, I believed we could leave right then and there. Hit the road and never come back. But who were we kidding? I shrugged.

Curtis flexed his hands on the wheel. "We're getting close."

"What are we looking for?" I asked.

"Some godforsaken road that leads to nowhere."

The side of the road rolled by in a blur: a long wire fence, an old church, a ranger station, a deserted gas station. The tires cried as they bent, holding onto a lazy curve. I put my palm against the door to steady myself.

"Hey, Curtis," Bruce said. "I think you need a high school diploma to get into Canada. I guess that leaves you out."

Curtis looked at Bruce in the rearview mirror and gave him the finger.

Bruce laughed.

Bruce and I had both graduated from high school a couple of weeks ago. Curtis had some time to make up in summer school. He was lucky to have the chance, really. The school year started off pretty bad for him; his dad died in September. His heart finally gave out on him. He never had much of one to begin with. But Curtis went kind of nuts after that. I couldn't understand why. His dad treated Curtis like crap, always bitching at him. He could never do anything right.

The only thing they had in common was Elvis. Curtis was raised on Elvis. I sure wasn't. My dad was tone-deaf, I think. The only thing he ever listened to was some stupid Herb Alpert eight-track he kept in his station wagon. But Curtis got me to listen to Elvis, and my life was never the same.

While all the other kids were banging their heads against the air to Led Zeppelin, Queen, AC/DC, bands like that, and calling them gods of rock and roll, me and Curtis, we were different. For us, it was all about Elvis.

Since he died in August 1977, I had become fascinated with him. Not that his dying had anything to do with it. But I remember the headline that day: "Elvis Presley, Rock Singing Star, Dies." In the days that followed, stories about Elvis filled the papers. There were pictures of thousands of people gathered outside of Graceland, hoping to see him one last time or touch his casket; pictures of women bawling their eyes out the day they buried him.

People believed in him. They believed in him to a point that went beyond what he was as a person, went beyond what was real, what was credible in this world. He was pure. He touched them at a deep level. For me, it was the way he sang. His voice. There was something about it, like it was coming from some better place. I don't know. I loved listening to him.

Sometimes, when Curtis's dad was out of the house, we snuck into his den and listened to his Elvis records. He had about a million of them. We were always careful, though, and put the records back exactly where we found them, or Curtis would pay for it. At least he had something that bonded him with his dad. My dad cut out on my mom and me when I was twelve. I didn't miss him. I hardly ever spoke to him anymore. People adapt.

But Curtis took his dad's death pretty hard. Curtis used to say that suicide was never the answer, but sometimes it was the solution. I thought he was kidding until he tried it. A bunch of rumors went around school. I heard that he took a bunch of his mom's pills, and I heard that he slit his wrists and held them over the toilet, and I heard that he tried to hang himself from his dad's ham radio antennae. All I knew for sure was that the ambulance pulled up to his house with its rollers on and took him away. I never asked him what happened. I didn't think he wanted to talk about it. Wasn't sure I did either. I never saw any scars on his wrists.

After that, they put Curtis in this mental place in Tampa. They said it was a school. Yeah, a school with bars on the windows and locked doors. I visited him almost every week, but sometimes he wouldn't even talk to me. He'd just sit there, staring off.

I can't see killing yourself, no matter how bad things get. It's not like I didn't think about it every now and then; I guess everybody feels bummed out, hopeless. I don't know. But I know that after Curtis got out, we didn't talk about it.

"Is that it?" I pointed to a dirt road off the highway.

"Yeah." Curtis clamped on the brakes. The tires groaned against the rough asphalt. He cut the wheel. The front tires bit into the limestone road and the back of the car crunched sideways, then whipped straight. Bruce was thrown across the back seat and slammed into the cooler.

The Dart rumbled over the rough white limestone that glowed in the moonlight. We hit a pothole that rattled the broken glass inside the passenger door. A few weeks ago when we were messing around with our BB guns, I'd managed to clip the top edge of the window. It shattered inside the door.

Curtis accelerated. I felt my eyes swell as I drew in a deep breath. The car seemed faster over the rough road. It rocked and bounced. A dense forest loomed ahead of us. The cypress and pine trees were so thick the white road emerged from them like a tongue from the throat of darkness. My stomach thrilled as the car dipped and then rose. We seemed to fly through the air as we plunged into the pitch-black woods.

The road became a blur racing beneath our headlights. It twisted and bent. I put one hand on the dash and one on the door, trying to hold myself in place, bracing myself for anything. It was like riding in a mine cart on a crazy free fall to the center of the earth.

"This is nuts!" Bruce spread his arms wide across the back seat. "Slow down!"

Curtis didn't slow down at all; his eyes narrowed with focus. I leaned forward, searching the road ahead. I was afraid we would hit something or Curtis would lose control of the car or the road would take a turn he couldn't react to. Branches flashed through our headlights and seemed to grope at us from the side of the road. An opening appeared ahead of us. My eyes locked on it. I hoped we would make it through, make it back out into the moonlight. Curtis sped toward it. I blew out my breath as we burst out.

The road veered sharply. The car broke free, leaping over the edge and bounding across a field. Curtis jammed on the brakes. The car twisted sideways. I reached forward, clutching the dash. Dirt sprayed in through the window as the wheels scraped across the earth. Bruce tumbled off the seat onto the floor. The cooler landed on him, spilling beer and ice everywhere.

A thick cloud of dirt rolled past us. It swept over our eyes. I put my hand up to shield my face. Curtis and I sat there, waiting for the air to clear. Bruce was coughing, hacking out dirt clods.

"You could've gotten us killed!" Bruce lifted himself off the floor and back onto the seat. "Look at this frigging mess." He shoved what ice he could back into the cooler.

The top of my beer can was covered with dirt. I tossed it out the window. Curtis did the same. He reached back, took two beers off the floor, and handed me one. We got out.

"What the hell's wrong with you?" Bruce brushed off his pants and arms. "And where are we staying? Where is this cabin?"

Curtis pointed toward the edge of the clearing. "Over there."

A misshapen lump sat in a scattering of cypress trees. It looked like a black tumor nested in darkness.

"You're kidding, right?"

"Nope," Curtis said.

Bruce put his hands on his hips and shook his head. "Holy crap."

"It looks better up close," Curtis said.

"It would have to."

Curtis and I climbed up on the trunk and lay back on the window. We looked at the stars above us. Bruce kept chattering away, mostly bitching at Curtis. I didn't hear a word. Curtis sure as hell wasn't paying any attention. Finally, Bruce shut up and started rummaging through the trunk for our lantern.

The moon sat high above the clearing. I stared up at it. Now that it was over, there was something about that moment. We had faced it all and made it through. Yeah, Curtis had gotten crazy and almost killed us, but he didn't. And even though his driving scared the crap out of me, there was a part of me that was into it. That got charged when he pulled his crap. I put my hands behind my head. Everything was quiet. Peaceful. I could've laid there the rest of the night. We had broken out and entered into a world separate from anything we had known, a place that was all our own. It felt like the stars were reaching out to me, connecting with me somehow.

I took a sip of my beer and searched the scarred surface of the moon.

"Well, we made it," Curtis said. "Canada!"

I almost fell off the trunk from laughing so hard.

# *Breaking Out*

The car ride wasn't the end of it that night. I wish it was. But there was more. Curtis did almost get us all killed again. And that was bad, but it wasn't the worst thing that happened. What really set us off, what put us on the run, was something else. Sometimes you don't know the significance of something you do until it's too late, too late to take it back, too late to do anything about it except ride it out. Like missing that first step at the top of the stairs and taking that long, end-over-end tumble down. All you can do is think: "*Whoops! I shouldn't've done that.*"

Because I can't help but think, but *know*: if we hadn't broken into that trailer, none of that crazy ride that started the next day ever would've happened. Things would've been different. But maybe not. Maybe it still would've all ended the same.

But I can't defend what we did. Busting into that trailer was wrong. I knew that as we did it, and I knew it afterward. I know it now. Somehow that didn't matter. Maybe it was the beer. Maybe it was the moon. Maybe it was because we were going to do whatever the hell we wanted to do that night, because this was the last time the three of us would go off together, and nothing was going to stop us, or stop Curtis, anyway. Maybe I should blame those damn mosquitos.

•••••••••••

The wooden steps groaned as Curtis walked up to the door of the cabin. I stood on the ground and held the lantern. It sputtered and hissed, casting a wavering light on the weathered boards that jutted unevenly from the walls. Some hung at odd angles and lengths. Some were just leaned in place. Thick, milky plastic dangled in tatters from the windows.

I looked back to our car on the other side of the clearing. That trailer sat behind it along the far edge of the trees. It looked pretty decent; looked like the Taj Mahal compared to what we were going to bed down in.

"Crap!" Bruce slapped at his neck. "I'm getting eaten alive."

"Quit your whining." I killed a mosquito sucking at my arm.

Curtis turned the wooden block holding the door shut and opened it. He poked his head in, then pulled it out. "Come on with the light."

I brushed past Bruce and plunged the lantern into the cabin. Long shadows stretched up the gray walls. Four cots with dingy, blue-striped mattresses sat on the plank floor. A cypress knee had pushed its way through one of the floorboards in the back corner below a glossy picture of a naked blonde chick spreading her legs and fingering herself. I looked at Curtis.

"That shit don't mean nothing." Curtis started saying that a few months back. I think he picked it up in that mental place. He said it any time he found appropriate. There were quite a few. A few times, Bruce pointed out that it was a double negative. Curtis didn't care, and Bruce gave up that crusade. I even heard Bruce say it once or twice. Eventually, the phrase got reduced to "Don't mean nothing." And if Curtis said it, then I would say, "That shit." And vice versa.

The cabin was about as nice as I thought it would be. I left. I had no interest in hanging out in it. At least I wouldn't have to deal with sleeping in there for a few more hours and a few more beers.

"Where's the Off?" Bruce slapped at his shoulder. "This is miserable."

"In the trunk," Curtis said.

A fire pit sat in front of the cabin beside a bunch of palmettos. Logs were placed around the pit like benches. I hung the lantern on a nail in a nearby tree. Curtis dragged our cooler from the car.

Bruce rummaged through the trunk. "I can't find it." He swatted at the back of his leg.

Curtis went over to his car to help. He dug through his trunk and came up empty except for a flashlight.

"Damn." I smashed a mosquito on my neck. "I feel like a bag of suet."

"Let's go," Bruce said. "This sucks."

"I'm not going," Curtis said. "We just got here."

"Bruce is right," I said. "The mosquitos are too thick. This is going to be miserable if we don't have Off or something."

"No! We're not going," Curtis said.

"What do you suggest then?" Bruce asked

Curtis bit his lips. His eyes shifted. "I bet there's some in that trailer."

"What do you mean?" Bruce looked at Curtis. "What are you going to do?"

Curtis raised his eyebrows.

"You can't." Bruce shook his head.

There was a time when Bruce exerted some control over Curtis. But that time was long gone. That was when we first started hanging out together. I was never sure why, because Curtis sure never listened to anyone else. Maybe it was because of who Bruce was and his upbringing. Bruce had a perfect family. His dad was a lawyer. His mom was on the board of the PTA. And he was their perfect kid. Most of the time. Except when he hung out with us.

Curtis looked to me, "There isn't anybody here. We can do whatever we want. We can't give up. We can't get chased off by some damn bugs."

Bruce folded his arms across his chest. "I don't want anything to do with it."

"Come on." Curtis said to me. "Nobody's around. Who's going to know?"

"It's not worth it, Curtis. Damn!" Bruce and Curtis stared at each other.

Curtis's crap was getting old to Bruce. He had his head set on college next year. Gainesville. His father went there, and I think even his father's father. In a way, I envied him: he knew where he was heading and probably what he was going to do when he got there. That was a lot more than I could say.

Mostly, I wanted to get away, just go somewhere. There wasn't anyone, besides Curtis, that I had any plans of seeing again. Most of them were assholes. That's how I met Curtis. Three assholes had me pinned up against a wall. They were juniors. I was a sophomore. I was fat back then too. A lot of kids ragged on me because of it. That kind of stuff can make you feel shitty about yourself after a while. That day they were trying to shake me down for my pack of smokes just to be dicks. Curtis came along and told them to piss off, which they did. I don't blame them. Curtis was a pretty big guy. After they left, Curtis told me what a dumbass I was for smoking. I couldn't really argue. We were friends from that day on. I admired him. He was someone who said exactly what he thought. No bullshit. I felt better about myself hanging out with Curtis. He didn't judge me. He didn't try to make me feel shitty about myself. Everything seemed all right when we were hanging out.

But that was back then. Now I didn't know where Curtis's head was at, and I didn't know where I was going. All I knew was that I either needed to start school in the fall or go out and get a job. And neither of those prospects looked very attractive. Maybe that's why these weekend trips that we took were the only thing that I looked forward to. They gave me something to head toward, something to want. Kept me from feeling so damn restless all the time. For a little while, anyway.

"I'm doing it." Curtis walked toward the trailer.

I went after him.

Curtis took a turn at the door handle. It was locked. There was a window next to the door, the kind that you crank out.

He took his buck knife from his belt, slid it under one of the glass panels, and pried it open. The two of us dug our fingers into the gap and yanked on it. One of the hinges snapped. The window panel wobbled down on the one good hinge. I looked to Curtis. He shrugged. He reached around, unlocked the door, and walked in. I stood there frozen for a minute. I didn't want to go in. I didn't want to cross that line.

The other things that we had done had always been to ourselves, at our own risk. This was different. This was wrong. This was doing something to someone else, whether we needed bug spray or not. And I knew, to Curtis, it was about more than the bug spray. This was crossing a line we hadn't crossed before. Curtis kept pushing things further and further.

But I followed after him.

Curtis snapped on the kitchen light. The inside of the trailer was nice. It looked like a grandma or an old aunt had decorated it. It looked liked a home. Curtains hung in the window. Knickknacks and family pictures rested on the end tables. I rummaged through the cabinets in the kitchen. I found a can of Off under the sink and held it up for Curtis.

"Great," Curtis said. "See? Problem solved."

"Okay, let's get out of here."

"What's your hurry? I'm going to the bedroom and see what else we can find."

I made my way back to the door and stopped in the living room. One of the walls was mirrored. An oil painting of Elvis reflected in it. He was young, wearing a loose yellow shirt and holding a microphone. He wasn't singing or anything. He just stared ahead. That was the thing about Elvis, his eyes. Even in that picture, those eyes were still looking, looking right at me, seeing through me into the core of my heart. I thought about all the people that believed in him, and, if there was a heaven or anything like that, he could have been looking at me right then. Seeing into my soul. Seeing what we were doing. I straightened. I felt shitty about myself. "Let's get out of here."

"Jackpot!" Curtis said. He walked out of the bedroom. "I found a box of bullets."

"Come on. Let's go." I grabbed him by the shirt and pulled him after me.

"Okay, okay."

We went back to the cabin. Bruce sat on one of the logs in front of the fire pit. He watched as we approached. I sprayed myself with Off and then tossed it to him.

Curtis and I piled dried palm fronds and small sticks in the pit. I put in a cassette tape, Skynyrd. That was a staple for us on nights like these. The live album. Curtis tossed on a cup of white gas and then ignited it. He put the can beside the cooler and set the cap on top. The palm fronds burned hot and bright. We threw on some more sticks and then a few big logs. Curtis dumped on another cup of white gas with a burst. I felt a charge watching the flames grope the air.

Skynyrd wailed out "Freebird" and Curtis started doing mouth-jams, holding out his hands like he was playing a guitar and trying to sing like one. My blood pumped. In the shadowy light, Curtis danced around the fire. He had his head thrown back, and his feet pounded the ground as he circled the pit. I danced around like a madman with him.

The fire raged, logs snapping and crackling. It felt like electricity was surging through me. Curtis stopped on the opposite side of the flames from Bruce and me. He held up the box of bullets, opened them, raising his hands above his head as if presenting an offering. He dumped them into the middle of the blaze. I stopped dead. I couldn't believe what he had done. Sometimes Curtis took things too far. He didn't know when to stop.

"Are you out of your mind?" Bruce stood up.

Curtis started dancing again like he didn't care what happened, didn't care whether he got shot, like he didn't know that in a minute or so hot lead was going to start shooting through the air. In some ways, when I was with Curtis, I felt that I was watching a drowning man. I wanted to grab him and shake him and ask him what the hell he was thinking.

Bruce ducked behind a tree.

"Curtis, get behind a tree, man," I said. "The bullets are going to start going off soon."

Curtis kept dancing.

I went to him. I put my hand on his shoulder. "This is crazy. You're going to get shot." He brushed me off and kept going.

One bullet went off, then another one. They started going off like popcorn. Curtis didn't miss a step. One blew a chunk out of one of the pine trees. Embers sprayed across the ground. I ran behind a tree. Glowing red shoots of flame spread through the dry pine needles. Bullets kept exploding every couple of seconds. Curtis circled the fire, oblivious to it all. His arms flailed through the air; his body was a wild silhouette in the flickering orange light.

The can of Coleman gas sat beside the cooler. The cap rested at an angle on the opening. The burning pine needles were inching closer. If the flames reached the can and caught the vapors coming from it, the whole forest would go up in a white-hot blast. Curtis's head rocked back and forth. He stomped around the campfire. The flames started licking at the base of the can. I ran for it, hoping like hell it didn't blow up. One bullet burst. I picked the can up, grabbed the cap, and screwed it down. *Bam!* Another went off. I looked down at my chest, expecting to see a hole with blood gushing from it. I ran toward the tree I came from. *Bam!* I got behind it and leaned back against the rough bark. My heart was hammering, and I struggled to catch my breath. I set the can down. Another bullet popped.

The bullets diminished to sporadic blasts before stopping altogether. Bruce and I got out from behind the trees and stomped out the little fires fingering out across the pine needles.

Curtis stopped his dance. He leaned forward with his hands on his knees. "Damn," he said. His chest was heaving for breath. He muttered something I couldn't quite make out. It might've been, "I showed you." He straightened up, closing his eyes and drawing in a deep inhale through pursed lips. A look of calmness came over him. He rocked his head back and blew out.

Sparks burst from the fire and shot across the ground in a line. Bruce jumped, putting his hand to his chest.

Curtis laughed at him. "Turn around. I want to see if you wet your pants."

"Screw you! You're lucky we didn't end up getting shot." Bruce glared at Curtis. His teeth were clenched, and he was puffing like he had just run a mile or something. "You could've blown up the whole damn forest."

Curtis shrugged.

Bruce leaned in toward Curtis. "I don't get you. You're a damn nutcase. Talking about your dad like you and him were best buddies, talking about him wanting to take you fishing in Canada. Your dad wouldn't have pissed on your head if your hair were on fire, and you know it."

"Don't say shit about my dad." Curtis stuck out his chest and took a step toward Bruce.

"None of us bought that story about the burn on your arm."

I stepped between them and put my hand on Curtis's chest.

"Hit your arm on a stove burner. Hmm, that doesn't explain how it was perfectly round." Bruce cocked his head. "Your dad used to smoke cigars, didn't he?"

Curtis pushed forward against me, trying to get at Bruce. I wrapped my arms around him. "Settle down, Curtis." I held him back. "It's not worth it." As big as Curtis was, he could've knocked me away like a paper doll if he wanted to.

Bruce picked up the flashlight and walked to the cabin. "I don't know why I even came with you guys. You don't listen to anything. You're a couple of losers."

I let Curtis go, grabbed two beers out of the cooler, and handed one to him. He sat on a log by the fire. He put his elbows on his knees and rested his head in between his hands, jabbing his fingers through his bushy hair. We sat there in silence.

The campfire burned down, low and red. Our Coleman lantern hissed in spasms. Small moths looped through the air around it. Curtis drew back on his tall boy. In the firelight, rough shadows stretched across his scarred knuckles. He leaned back and picked up a handful of pine needles. He threw them one by one into the fire. They burned bright, then shriveled to nothing.

"We did get kind of wild tonight," I said.

Curtis nodded. He tossed another needle into the fire. A big moth thumped against the lantern glass. "Bruce was wrong about my dad." He lifted his gaze from the fire and looked me in the eye.

"I know." But I knew that Bruce wasn't wrong about Curtis's dad. Not at all.

"My dad could be a jerk. But—"

"We acted crazy tonight." I shook my head.

"Yeah, I did, anyway. I guess that's why they put me in that loony bin."

"What was it like in there?"

"Have you ever seen a porta-potty?"

"Yeah."

"It was like living under one of those." He threw a pine needle into the fire like a spear. "It's funny. I still feel him around sometimes."

"Your dad?"

"Yeah." Curtis scraped a handful of pine needles off the ground and threw them on the fire. They writhed like snakes and melted. He looked up at the moon. "I don't give a shit. I'm past that. I'm free of all that." He smiled. "That don't mean nothing."

"That shit."

"I proved that tonight."

I nodded. But what had he really proved, that he could push things further than he had before and still survive? And what would he do next weekend? Look for the next big thrill. Push things even further. When would that end? When he was dead? When we were both dead? I could see how torn up he was. He was my best friend and I would've done anything for him. I would've given him anything that I had, but I couldn't give him what he really needed: peace in his heart.

We sat there until the fire burned down to blood-red embers, pulsating brighter then darker as they faded beneath ash. The last foamy drops of my beer hissed as I dumped them on the fire. Curtis and I got up. I took the lantern off the tree, and we went to the cabin. We each took a bunk. Bruce snored lightly. I lay on my back, smelled the smoke, and thought of nothing but the fire and the embers and the huge moon watching it all.

# Rude Awakening

I woke up dreaming about mosquitos whining around my ear. They just wouldn't go away. They kept whining. Whining and whining. They pulled me out of my sleep until I was awake enough to realize that I wasn't dreaming. And that it wasn't mosquitos at all. It was voices. People chattering. Then I thought I was home. But I opened my eyes, rolled over, and looked out the window. Between the flapping tatters of milky plastic in the window, I saw a car parked out there, and this old guy and woman, the same people I saw in one of the pictures in that trailer Curtis and I busted into, walking around. I knew where I was then. I just wished I was home.

The woman saw me peeking out the window and pointed. I rolled off the bed and crawled across the floor toward Curtis. He lay on his back with his mouth wide open, snoring like Rip Van Winkle. Bruce lay on his side against the wall, snoring about as bad.

I grabbed Curtis by the shirt and shook him. "Get up, man. There are some people walking around the trailer." He turned over. His eyes popped open wide. Bruce sat up. Curtis and I crawled to my bunk, and we peeked out.

The old guy stood by his tank of a car, some old-man kind of car, maybe a Town Car. His hands were on his hips. A pistol hung in a holster around his waist.

Bruce got up and paced, careful to stay out of view of the windows. His gaze shifted around the cabin like he was searching for something, maybe a hole to crawl into. "What are we going to do?" He shook his head. "I knew you guys shouldn't have broken into that trailer."

"Shut up." Curtis buried his face in his hands. "I don't believe this." He looked at me. "I'm not going to jail."

The old guy walked over to our car and wrote down our license plate.

"They're going to report us to the cops. We've got to do something. Maybe we should go over and talk to them," I said.

"What are we going to say?" Curtis asked. "Are we going to ask them about the weather or what?"

"What do you think we should do? Tunnel our way out of here?" I snapped back. "Or maybe you think they'll just go away and forget about it."

Curtis shook his head. "They might go away. But if they do, they're going to report us to the cops for sure. Damn." He kicked the leg of the bunk. "You're right. We've got to go over and talk to them."

"What are we going to say?" Bruce said, eyes blinking like a strobe light.

"I don't know," I said. "Let's see what they say to us first."

"Good plan," Bruce said. His voice dripped with sarcasm.

"Shut up," I said.

We marched out of the cabin. I led the way. The old man turned and looked at us like Clint Eastwood in one of those westerns. His wife stood there with her arms crossed. She had short, curly hair and black horn-rimmed glasses. The old guy was mostly bald, and his head was dotted with brown spots. He put his hand on the butt of his gun. It was something small, maybe a .22. "You boys broke that window. Didn't you?" He tilted his head up and looked down his nose at us.

"Did something happen to your window?" I asked.

"You fellows know darn well something happened to our window." The old man folded his arms across his chest. Circles of sweat spotted each of his armpits. "You fellows look guilty as can be."

"What makes you say that?" Curtis cocked his head to the side.

"You wouldn't have been hiding in that shack if you weren't guilty of something." His wife pointed at us. "We saw you, ducking and peeking at us." Her thin lower lip was curled slightly down; her mouth looked like a frog's.

"Hiding? We were sleeping," I said.

"Look, we'll pay for the window." Bruce stepped in front of me. "We can just forget about this whole thing."

"Why do you want to pay for it, if you didn't even break it in the first place?" the man asked. He looked hard at Bruce.

There was a long silence. Bruce melted under his stare. He broke down. "I didn't have anything to do with it. I told them not to."

Curtis and I glared at him.

The old man smiled. "What did you think you were going to accomplish by breaking in?"

"The mosquitos were real bad," I said. "We wanted to find some Off or something."

"Mosquitos? That's a crock." His eyes bore in on me.

"We'll pay for the window," I said. "We didn't bust anything up."

"Oh, so you'll pay for it." The old man leaned back and raised his chin. "Who would've paid for it if we hadn't caught you? Worthless teenage punks. Look at your fire pit. It looks like you about burned down the forest last night. And don't think I didn't notice all the empty beer cans around your campsite. You boys probably aren't even old enough to drink. The sheriff of this county is a good friend of mine."

"We're sorry." Bruce bowed his head. "Can't we just pay for the window and forget it?"

"I don't think so."

"So what happens now?" I asked.

The old man paused. Truth was he didn't know what the hell to do with us. He and his wife walked a short distance away to talk without us being able to hear them.

A locust screamed from the top of one of the pine trees. It sounded like a buzz saw. Bruce paced, shaking his head back and forth and mumbling to himself.

Curtis leaned against his car with his arms folded across his chest. "We've got to get out of here. I'm not going to jail. They'll put me back in that psycho ward."

"Man, they got your license plate," Bruce said. "And we'll get in more trouble for taking off."

"We're in trouble anyway. But at least they'll have to catch us," Curtis said.

I didn't know what I wanted to do. All I knew was that it sure was hot standing out in the sun and no matter what we did, it wouldn't be the right thing to do. That ship had sailed. They walked back toward us.

"Okay, I'm going to take you boys in myself." The old man stuck out his chest. He saw himself as a hero on the six o'clock news, bringing in us dangerous criminals.

Curtis shook his head. "You aren't taking us in. We told you we'd pay for the window. Come on, let's get out of here." He started toward his car. I followed him. Bruce stood there.

"You aren't going anywhere, son." The old man stepped into Curtis's path. "Two of you get in my car. The other one can follow us in your car." He took out his gun and pointed it at Curtis. "Get in the car."

"Get that gun out of my face." Curtis waved his hand through the air, taking a swat at it.

The old guy took a step back. His mouth opened funny. He was stunned. His expression hardened and went toward Curtis. He reached out to grab his shirt. "You're coming with me."

Curtis knocked his arm away. "Don't touch me."

The old guy staggered back a step.

"Don't you have any respect?" his wife asked Curtis.

The old guy started yelling at us, calling us punks and delinquents and a whole bunch of other names. His face got bright red. I thought the vein on the side of his forehead was going to have a blowout. He waved the gun around in the air. Curtis screamed back at him. His fists were clenched tight. I wished like hell I was any place else.

The old man kept yelling, but his tone changed; he wasn't as sure of himself as before. There was a yelp to it, like he was a little dog barking at a big dog. Spit sputtered from his mouth. The whole time, he kept the gun pointed at Curtis's gut. "Get in the car," he said, over and over.

Curtis slapped at the gun. "Put that gun away!"

The old guy took a step toward Curtis. "You do what I tell you. Get in my goddamned car!"

"No!" Curtis said, his face clenched and red. He was puffing. He grabbed the end of the gun and drove forward into him, pushing him back. The old guy stumbled and fell. Curtis landed on top of him. The old guy rolled over, but Curtis twisted around and knocked him into the dirt. Both of them were grabbing at the gun, rolling around on the ground, stirring up dust and flailing their arms and legs. There was so much dirt flying and so many limbs kicking, it was hard to follow the gun until it went off.

Curtis scrambled off the guy like he was on fire. Curtis jumped to his feet, the gun in his hand. The old guy's mouth opened wide as he stared down at himself. A large red stain spread across the middle of his white polo shirt.

"You shot me."

The image of that old guy seared into my mind. His eyes bulging. His face twisted in confusion and pain and shock. And that blood. Man, that blood, growing across his shirt.

Curtis staggered back a step. Bruce's face went stiff like it had set in cement. I was sure my face looked about the same. My hand was shaking as I brought it to my mouth. How could things have gotten so bad so fast?

The lady knelt beside her husband. Her head wobbled, and her chin was trembling. I wanted to run. Run and run and never look back. Run so far and fast that this could never catch up with us.

Curtis stared at the gun in his hand.

I went to him. "Curtis." He looked at me; his eyes were wild. "Snap out of it."

"It hurts," the old guy said. "God, it hurts."

"We've got to get out of here," Curtis said.

"No…we've got to . . ." Bruce stumbled toward us. He was white as a ghost. "We've got to . . ." His head quivered back and forth like a bobble-head doll.

"You've got to help us." Tears rolled down the lady's face. "I need to get him to a hospital."

Bruce went forward and grabbed Curtis by the shirt. "This is all your damn fault!" He shook him.

I stepped forward and yanked Bruce back. "Back off."

"I guess it is." Curtis stared off at something a mile away.

The old guy groaned. His hand lay across his midsection. He dug his foot into the ground as if trying to kick himself away from his pain.

His wife stroked his forehead. "It's going to be all right. I'm going to take care of you."

"Let's help him into the car," I said.

"No. No. No," Curtis said. "They've got our license plate number." He looked up at the guy and his wife. "We could just . . ." He was unable to finish saying what he was thinking.

"What are you talking about?" I asked.

"I'm going to…" Curtis cradled the gun in his hands. He nodded his head like he was trying to convince himself of something.

What he was trying to say hit me. We were out in the middle of nowhere. Miles from any place. If we decided to finish things, who would've known except us? I moved toward him. I couldn't let it go any further than the way too far it had gone already. I couldn't let it go that far. No matter how scared Curtis was. I had to stop him, and I had to get Curtis out of this. I had to get him away from these people. He took a step toward them, the gun at his side.

"You stay away from us." The old guy put up his hand, his fingers trembling.

I moved in front of Curtis. "Man, let's get in the car and go."

"I can't go to jail."

"What are you guys even talking about?" Bruce said. His voice was cracking. I thought he was going to cry, not that I would've blamed him.

"Give me the gun." I held my hand out to Curtis.

"If we let them go, the cops are going to pick us up before we can get ten miles." Curtis lifted the gun from his side and pointed it at the old couple. "We've got to…we've got to . . ." His hand shook.

"Leave us alone!"

"We can't do this." I put myself in front of the gun, placed my hand on the barrel and pushed it down. I moved in closer to Curtis. "Come on. Just give it to me."

Curtis's eyes blinked as he looked past me. His lips were clenched and quivering. His head sank, and he nodded. I took the gun from him, clicked on the safety and tucked it under my belt.

The old guy lay on the ground with his wife kneeling next to him. "We're going to help you into your car." The old guy nodded. His wife kept her head bent to the ground.

The old guy moaned in pain as Bruce and I helped him to his feet. We got him into the backseat of their car. The lady drove off. Their car disappeared into the forest, leaving a trail of white dust.

# Mile Marker 0

We threw our stuff in the car and drove back out through the woods, emerging into blazing sunlight. That limestone road was so damn bright it scalded my eyes. And that pistol was jammed down my jeans, digging into my gut. I slid it over and caught a whiff of the burnt gunpowder.

I kept running that acid scene through my head: that old man yelling at us, Curtis losing it, the two of them wrestling around, the gun going off. It played over and over.

Bruce twisted on the seat and looked out the back window, checking to see if anyone was chasing us. As if there were a chance. "I don't believe that happened, man." He turned to face us. He looked like Costello after he laid eyes on Frankenstein's monster. "What are we going to do?"

"Shit!" Curtis yelled.

I snapped my head over.

"Damn thing is jabbing me." He jerked his buck knife out of the leather case on his belt and tossed it on the dash, then ran his fingers through his hair.

Bruce wobbled his head and closed his eyes. "I never should've come with you guys. I never should've come with you guys. I never should've come with you guys." I thought he was going to start banging his heels together like Dorothy or something.

"Damn! I'm so tired of listening to you bitch and moan," Curtis said. "Do you need a Valium or something?"

"I don't believe this. I don't believe this." Bruce paused.

"Does somebody have to slap you?" I asked.

Bruce nodded. "Yeah, that might be good?"

"Sure." I turned around in the seat and cuffed Bruce across the chops. I hit him pretty hard too.

"I meant a Valium."

Curtis smiled.

"Damn, you didn't have to hit me so hard." Bruce rubbed his jaw. "The whole thing last night was stupid. It was even stupider not to give in to whatever they wanted us to do. They caught us red-handed."

"No, they didn't. You told them, you bonehead." Curtis glared at Bruce in the rearview mirror. "We could've talked our way out of it. If you'd kept your mouth shut."

Bruce met Curtis's gaze. "They had us. They knew it was us."

"They couldn't've proved it." Curtis shifted his eyes back to the road.

I shook my head. "What are we going to do?" I asked. No one said anything. "What are we going to do?" I repeated softly to myself.

The car picked up speed as it rattled over the road. The tires crunched, crushing stones into the chalky road, spitting a few up. One clanged off the underside of the car.

Curtis's buck knife vibrated on the dash like a bee on speed trapped under a shot glass.

I noticed a splotch of blood on Curtis's Jethro Tull T-shirt, right in the center of his gut. It looked like a Rorschach inkblot, some kind of a bat or a mutant butterfly. "Curtis, you got some blood on you, man." I pointed at it.

He looked down. "Oh, Jesus." He squirmed, pushing back into his seat, eyes wide. He pawed at his shirt. Curtis yanked it off over his head while I grabbed the wheel. "Get me one out of my bag," he yelled back to Bruce.

"Calm down, Curtis," I said. "It's okay."

Curtis threw the bloody shirt out the window. It floated down into the ditch along the side of the road. Curtis pulled on a fresh one, then took the wheel.

The tires strained as he rounded a curve. The few remaining beers sloshed against the side of the cooler. Bruce grabbed the headrest behind me to steady himself.

Curtis hit that long straightaway back to Highway 41 and floored it. Jet trails of white dust swelled behind us. We closed in on the black asphalt of the highway. Curtis ground the car to a stop at the intersection. A white dust cloud pushed past us. Palmetto scrub stretched away from us in every direction. The car chugged at idle.

No one was coming in either way. We were at the turn we took last night. Although last night seemed a long time ago, like it was part of another life. Curtis glanced south back toward home and then looked north.

Bruce leaned forward and stuck his face up between us. "What the hell are you doing? We head left. Back home! What the fuck else are we going to do?"

"Nope." Curtis shook his head. "I don't think so."

"What do you mean?"

"There's nothing there for me."

He was right about that. When it all came down, he had no one that would go to bat for him. His mom wouldn't help him. She was the one who had him put away in the first place. She would be leading the chorus against him, raining judgment down on him. He would be locked up. Without a doubt. Not that he didn't deserve it.

Bruce's father was a lawyer in Tampa. He was connected. The minute Bruce got home, his perfect mom would fix him some perfect cookies and milk while his dad got on the phone and took care of things. Made it all better. Kept him on his path.

At least my mom was almost normal, not that I ever let her know that. Mostly, I was crappy to her. I was in some trouble, but I wasn't worried about me as much as I was about Curtis. Maybe I should've been. I didn't think about how this all affected me. Somehow I didn't think it could pull me in the way it did. I felt immune to it. Like I was just a spectator, just along for the ride. That was stupid to think.

Curtis looked at me. "I can't go back. I'm not going back."

I knew he meant it. My eyes narrowed as I looked at him. I knew how hopeless the chances of getting away were. Where were we going to go, really? How far could we get before it all came crashing down on us, on him? Some things you can't escape. Some things you can't run away from. This was one of them. They had our license plate. They knew what we looked like. What did it matter whether we spent a few days aimlessly trying to get away? It was pointless. We didn't have much money. We didn't have any food.

Bruce shook his head. "We've got to go back home."

"No! Nothing's going to make me." Curtis looked to Bruce in the mirror. "You tell me—if that old man dies, what are we looking at? I'm not sure, but I'm guessing murder."

"We? You're the one that pulled the trigger," Bruce said.

"It was an accident." I turned to face Bruce.

"Yeah, I guess I did." Curtis's expression hardened. He shook his head and stared at the road, his lips pressed tight together.

He looked scared. Lost. Like in that moment, he had thought through every possible outcome for him, thought through everything that I had, and come to the same conclusion: he was fucked. He sunk his head against the steering wheel. I wanted to help him. But I didn't know what I could do or say or if there was anything. I wished I could've turned back time to before anything happened, before we broke into that trailer, before we even set out from home. But we were stuck with where we were, stuck living with what happened back there in the woods. You can't take things back.

Bruce flopped back against the seat and crossed his arms. "Not going back. That's stupid. Running is only going to make it worse."

Curtis lifted his head and looked up the road, north, to where it vanished behind the wavering vapor that rose from it. He never once glanced the other way. "I'm not going back. I'll do whatever I have to to keep from getting caught. We can let you out, Bruce. You can make your way home."

Bruce said nothing. It was hot. The slight breeze felt like a hair dryer blowing through the car. A line of sweat ran down my back. He nodded and looked down at his hands folded in his lap. "Okay."

Curtis turned to me. "What about you? Like Bruce said. I pulled the trigger."

"It will only take us a couple of hours to get back," Bruce said.

Going back was probably the right thing to do, and the smart thing. Face the music and get it over with. But what did I have back there for me? Curtis was about all I had in this world. As crazy as he was, he was my only true friend. I couldn't abandon him. And honestly, part of me wanted to go out on the road, wanted to get away from the shitty life I had back at home, to look for something better for myself out there someplace. As hopeless as it all was, maybe we could make it to Canada or some place away from here. Maybe we could find something out there. But I didn't know what that something would be. We had talked about it so much. This was our last chance to actually do it. And I knew that too. A part of me couldn't let that go.

"No, I'm not going back." I nodded to Curtis. "I'm staying."

He managed a weak smile.

"You're both nuts." Bruce hung his head. I thought he was going to start crying or something. That threw me. I thought Bruce was done with us, that this was the last straw. That he was leaving us and had no regrets. "I have to go back."

Curtis looked at me. "You should go back with Bruce. I'm the guy who had his hand on the gun. I'm the one that'll take the fall from this."

"It was an accident. Both of you were wrestling for the gun, and it just went off."

Curtis smiled. "I don't think the cops will see it like that."

Another reason I stayed was that I was afraid for Curtis. I knew he wouldn't come in easily. I thought that maybe I could keep him safe. I could somehow keep him under control when things started to go sideways. I could somehow protect him when the forces of, I don't know what you would call it, society, I guess, closed in on him. I didn't realize how hard it is to help the people who are the closest to you, especially when you're trying to protect them from themselves. You can try, but a lot of times you end up getting carried along on whatever mad scheme they have going.

Curtis eased the car forward. "We'll drop you when we get to the interstate. We haven't seen a car come by in five minutes. Besides, probably the next car to come by will be the cops going to the scene of the crime."

Bruce nodded.

Curtis headed north and rested his arm on his open window. We drove to the interstate in silence and dropped Bruce at the south-bound entrance ramp. I turned and watched him as we drove away. He shuffled up the ramp toward the southbound lane.

"I'm not going to miss him too much," Curtis said.

"Why's that?" I asked.

"He farts in his sleep. You should have heard him last night. He was like a fireworks display."

I laughed. Too much, really. Like I was going nuts for a minute. I thought I might need a Valium or a slap. Bruce shrank from my view as we drove away.

We headed north, toward the state line. We wanted to get out of Florida. We didn't know what we were doing. For some reason we thought that we would enter into another jurisdiction if we got out of the state. We were clueless. Our entire idea of how cops operated was derived from watching those *Dirty Harry* movies, *Perry Mason* reruns, and all those stupid cop shows on the tube.

The mile markers floated by our car like pegs on a raffle wheel. Curtis stared straight ahead, like he was looking beyond the road at some point miles into the distance that only he could see.

# Canada or Bust

The sharp edge we felt when we set out dulled with each mile. And with each mile, we became increasingly anxious, realizing that beyond getting out of the state we had no idea where to head. Curtis threw out Canada. No surprise there. But that seemed about as realistic as us making it to Mars, especially since we had a grand total of eighty-seven dollars between us. And with the fuel gauge easing its way below a quarter tank, we were about to make a dent in that. Canada? We'd be lucky to make it out of Georgia. Besides our meager funds, we each had a couple changes of clothes and a sleeping bag. We also had a Coleman lantern, a can of white gas, a jam box with dead batteries (we had left it on play all night), and a couple beers sloshing around in the cooler. That was pretty much our full inventory.

A strap of torn headliner hung from the ceiling. It waved in the breeze, snapping like a blunt whip. I pulled on it, tearing away a large swath.

"Make yourself at home," Curtis said.

"It was getting on my nerves."

We stopped at a 7-Eleven for gas. I went inside to get the pump turned on. The cashier was a tall, thin girl. She stood behind the counter, holding a carton of cigarettes and stuffing packs into an overhead rack.

"We need a fill-up," I called to her. She glanced toward me, then did a double take, straining to focus on me through Coke-bottle-thick glasses. She had an uneven smile; her two front teeth over-lapped. She finished emptying the carton and turned on the pump.

The magazine rack had a section of maps. I saw a couple of Florida; there were a few county maps and some that covered the entire Southeast. A United States atlas stood tall behind them. I picked it up and thumbed through it.

Curtis reached over my shoulder and snatched the atlas from me. He studied the cover. "That's exactly what we need." He dropped it back in my hands and scanned the magazines. "Grab some food too."

"What do you want?"

"Whatever. I don't care." Curtis picked up a fishing magazine with a picture of a guy holding a fly rod and standing in a mountain stream. "Look at this. This is about British Columbia." He held the magazine out for me. "This is a sign. Come on. Let's go there." He began to thumb through it, struggling to turn the slick pages. "That's it. That's where we're going. Canada. I'm getting this magazine."

"We need to be a little conservative with our cash."

"It's just three bucks."

"Maybe we should rob this place, because we aren't going to have any money once we get done here."

The cashier turned her head toward me then looked away.

"That girl is looking at me funny. You don't think the cops have already put out the word on us, do you?"

"You're being paranoid. Maybe she wants you."

I laughed uncomfortably. I wasn't exactly a Don Juan.

I saw a *National Enquirer* with a picture of Elvis on the cover. Underneath the picture was the caption: "Elvis's Love Child Found in Butte Orphanage." I chuckled as I picked it off the shelf. I nudged Curtis and held it out for him. He smiled at me, then went back to his fishing magazine.

Curtis and I loved reading the *Enquirer*. His mom used to buy it every week. I think she actually believed the stories. But when she was done, Curtis and I would sneak the magazine into his bedroom and read it cover to cover. It cracked us up. I remember one story about a bat-boy in Indiana who went on a murderous rampage and sucked the life out of seven people; another about the largest lady in Illinois who lived on a steady diet of Little Debbie's snack cakes, grape Nehi, and MoonPies.

Mostly we read it for the ones about Elvis. He may have died, but he sure didn't stay dead. He kept coming back, again and again. In one story, Elvis worked at a car wash in Albuquerque. In another, he was flopping Whoppers in Pittsburgh. In another, he had returned from spending time with space aliens with a brand-new diet. There were other stories about Elvis coming back as a ghost, appearing in someone's closet or at a truck stop or something like that.

The magazine always showed a picture of Elvis while he was on stage—his head bent down into his upturned collar, his face contorted and covered with sweat. Next to that would be a picture of Elvis flopping a Whopper, or a ghostly Elvis rifling through someone's closet or sitting in a booth at a truck stop diner, or Elvis with his arm around a bunch of aliens holding a platter of food from his diet. It was a riot. Elvis did more after he was dead than when he was alive.

Many of the stories suggested that he had faked his own death so he could escape his stardom and rock-and-roll lifestyle to live a simpler life. They made it out like he was now traveling around the country like the Lone Ranger. I'd like to believe that. Stranger things have happened in the world. Who knows? Maybe he was still out there on the road, going from place to place, helping people. You have to believe in something. Why not believe in Elvis out there, trying to make things better in some way?

Every week I visited Curtis in that mental place, I brought the

*Enquirer* and read it to him, read him stories about Elvis and all the strange people in the world. They cheered Curtis up. They cheered me up too. They helped us feel normal. That's a laugh. I guess normal compared to those people anyway.

I set the *Enquirer* back on the rack. I took the atlas and left Curtis. I picked up a few supplies: some potato chips, a can of chili, a few burritos, and a bag of ice. I popped two of the burritos into the microwave and went to the counter to pay.

As I approached the register, the cashier glanced at my belt line. She looked nervous as hell. She saw me catch her looking, and that freaked her out even more. I thought she was going to jump up to the ceiling. I didn't know what was going on. I thought maybe my pants were unzipped and Willy was hanging out. I looked down and about passed out. That stupid gun was tucked under my belt. I'd forgotten about it. I must've gotten used to it pressing against my gut. I guess it was the adrenaline or the confusion from all that happened. I couldn't believe I had done that. I felt so stupid.

"I don't want any trouble." She took a step back and put her hands up. "You can take what you want and leave."

"What are you talking about? I'm not going to give you any trouble." I moved my hand over the butt of the gun in a lame attempt to hide it. She backed away from the counter. I guess she thought I was reaching for it. I accidentally pushed the gun out from under my belt, and it dropped down into my pants and slid down my left pant leg, wedging sideways above my knee.

The girl froze. Her mouth opened in a crooked snarl. Her chin quivered. I thought she was going to start crying or something. I grabbed my pants and tried to shake the gun down my leg, but it was stuck.

Curtis came up and stood at the opening at the side of the register. The girl didn't notice him. She was intent on me and backed away to the far counter. She bent down toward the phone like she was going to pick it up. Curtis's eyes narrowed on her. He took a step toward her.

I wanted to yell, to tell her to stop, to tell Curtis to stop. We could just run and get out of there. We didn't need to cause any more trouble. I caught his gaze and scowled at him. His focus shifted back to the girl. Her glance wavered between the phone and me. Her hand started to reach for the phone. Curtis crept forward. I kept trying to shake that damn gun down my pant leg, but it wouldn't budge.

The bell on the door clanged. A woman with two young girls entered the store. Curtis stepped back. The cashier straightened. Curtis eased away and ducked behind one of the aisles out of view. The woman stood in front of me. She rested a hand on each of the girl's shoulders. They gaped at me.

"Are you all right?" she asked. She must've mistaken my twitching and shaking for some type of mental disorder or maybe a seizure. I wished it was that.

"He's got a gun!" the girl yelled. The words sprayed from her mouth like they had been jammed up inside her.

"Where?" The woman pulled her girls tight against her.

She pointed to my pants. "There!"

They all stared at the lump in my pants with horrified expressions. I can't say that felt like an unusual experience for me with women, but all I could think right then was how the hell did I get myself into this and how the hell could I get myself out. And where the hell did Curtis go and what was he planning to do now? I took a quick scan around the store, but I couldn't spot him. I wanted to get out of there as fast as I could. I felt I was sliding down a hill toward a deep chasm. I wasn't sure what I could do to stop it. A sweat broke across my forehead. The stiff odor of burned coffee cut the air and made me queasy.

Somehow I thought we were done with breaking the law. Somehow I thought Curtis wasn't going to lose it again like he had out in the woods. But by the look I saw on his face, I knew that wasn't the case. That was stupid for me to think. Like he said, he was going to do whatever he had to do to keep from getting caught.

I grabbed the gun through the fabric of my pants and wrestled the barrel to point downward. The gun slid past my knee and dropped to my ankle. The barrel popped out the opening of my pant leg, but the handle caught in the narrow end. I bent down and grabbed the barrel, twisting the gun free. The two little girls buried their faces into their mother's hip. I held the gun backwards with the handle pointing toward the cashier.

She looked at me. "Do you want me to give you the money?"

"No, I want…I want . . ." I turned that stupid gun and held it by the handle, careful not to point it at anyone. I motioned toward the register, trying to say that I wanted to pay for the stuff but nothing came out except some stuttering and stammering. I was so damn nervous. Between shooting that old man and this and the way Curtis was acting, I was about having a nervous breakdown. I still had no idea where he was.

She opened up the register. "Whatever you want." She pulled the bills out of their compartments and held them out for me.

"No, I just want to pay. I'm not robbing this place."

"Why do you have that gun in your hand then?" the woman asked.

"I was…ah . . ." I didn't have a good answer. I could've told them the truth—that we were on the run after shooting an old man, and I had stuffed it down there during the getaway. Somehow I didn't think that would help. I stood there like an idiot for what felt like an hour. Finally, I said. "It's not a real gun." I wasn't sure where I came up with that, but I had to say something. It was only thing I could think of.

"What do you mean?" the cashier asked.

"It's just a BB gun." I held it out for her to take a look.

She leaned her head toward it, taking a cautious look.

"Man." Curtis walked up. He seemed casual, relaxed. "I don't believe you."

He went toward me with his hand out, reaching for the gun, wanting to take it from me. I looked hard at him. I didn't want to give it to him. He was the last person I wanted to have the gun, but I couldn't start wrestling with him for it either. He put one hand on my shoulder and took the gun from my hand, pinching the butt between his index finger and thumb. There was nothing I could do without making a scene.

He held it and smiled. "Like he said, it's just a BB gun." He held it out for the cashier.

She still kept her distance. Her eyes stayed on the gun. I hoped she didn't look too closely, because it sure didn't look like a BB gun. Curtis smiled at her, but his teeth were clenched. He shifted his grip on the gun and held it by the handle, but kept it pointed away from her. I hoped like hell she believed us. I didn't know what I would do if she didn't. I didn't know what Curtis would do. I stood there waiting for her reaction. And that took about four hours.

"A BB gun?" She asked. She seemed to relax a bit and set the money back in the register.

Curtis lowered the gun to his side. He turned toward the door. "I'll take it back to the car. You don't have to worry about him. Even if he did try to shoot you, he'd probably miss. He hasn't hit anything all day."

"I'm sorry. I forgot I had it tucked in my jeans."

The cashier smiled weakly.

Curtis left the store. The woman walked off, giving me one last dirty look and pulling her girls with her. I paid, collected our stuff, and left. I dumped the ice into our cooler and put our food on top.

I got into the car. Curtis sat in the passenger's seat. "You were pretty smooth in there, Ace."

"Oh, shut up." I sat down behind the wheel and slammed the door shut.

"That was like watching a slow death."

"What the hell, Curtis?"

"What?"

I stared at him. He knew what I meant.

"Come on. Forget about it. We got out of it all right."

"What were you going to do anyway?"

"What do you mean?"

"When you were lurking behind that girl at the counter? When you took the gun out of my hand? What were you going to do?"

"I don't know. Something. I told you. I'll do whatever I have to."

"We can't take it too far like we did out in the woods."

"I'm not going back."

I kept my gaze on Curtis. "What'd you do with the gun?"

"I stuffed it under my seat." He picked up his magazine and began thumbing through it. "Did you warm up a couple burritos?"

"Oh, crap! I left them in the microwave."

"I guess you'd better go back."

I started the car. "I don't think so." I popped the car into drive and burned rubber pulling away from that store.

As I drove, Curtis put his feet up on the dash. He looked through his magazine and munched on a cold burrito. He read the parts of the magazine he liked out loud to me: "Ice-cold mountain-fed stream…rainbow trout as big as your arm…settling down at the end of the day to cook your fish over an open fire."

I sat there silently. I couldn't shake what had happened in that store. What would Curtis have done if the cashier had pushed it, if she had decided to call the cops? How far was he willing to go? I wished like hell we didn't have that damn gun. I couldn't let him hurt anyone else. I had to be ready to stop him the next time something like that happened. But what would that take? I doubted he would listen to me. No matter what, I couldn't let him hurt anyone else.

I wished I could find some way to help Curtis see the destructive path he was headed down. But how? How could I get him to see that he didn't need to choose that path? That he still had a chance in this world. That it wasn't too late for him. He was the closest person to me in my life. I didn't want to give up on him. And if I couldn't even help him, what did that make me?

He tossed the empty burrito wrapper behind him and set the magazine down on the seat between us. He leaned back, closed his eyes and smiled. "That would be the life. You know, when I was a kid, my dad took me fishing all the time, before he had all that heart trouble. He used to say that one day he was going to take me fishing in Canada. Like that guy in the magazine." Curtis rocked forward and thumped his finger on the guy fishing in a mountain stream on the cover. "I want to go there. Man, wouldn't that be cool? What's stopping us?"

Nothing was stopping us except for the fact we had no damn money, we were on the run, and that place was about three thousand miles away. We had about as much chance of making it to Canada as Frosty the Snowman had of making it through a two-week Caribbean cruise. I scowled at him, finding it hard to share his enthusiasm. "How are we going to make it there?"

"We'll find a way."

He ripped the glossy cover free of the magazine, grabbed his buck knife and opened it. He held the cover against the dashboard and plunged the knife into it, pinning the cover there. The knife barely stuck into the dash at the tip but held the cover in place. "That's where we're going. And nothing's getting in our way."

Article titles lined the left side: "Man Survives Wilderness for a Week after Attack by Grizzly," "10 Tips from Champion Fly Casters." A man probably in his forties stood at the edge of a stream holding a trout. Sunlight bounced off the drops of water that flew from the flopping fish. Mountains painted the horizon behind him, and, underneath that, a dense forest of pine trees lined the opposite bank of the stream. It looked perfect, too perfect. Phony. Something that had been airbrushed into existence. Something that was never real. The knife vibrated like it was charged with electricity.

"Canada or bust," Curtis said.

We hadn't gone twenty miles before the knife shook free and fell to the floor, taking the magazine cover with it.

# *Elvis Lives*

Curtis tracked our path north on the atlas with a red felt tip pen, marking each town and exit we passed. As the line drew closer to the Georgia border, a knot formed in my gut. I expected a roadblock at the state line: twenty state troopers angled toward us with their rollers on. Or maybe I thought some giant hand from above would thump down in front of us to stop us dead. But nothing happened. We just drove into Georgia.

It did feel like we were breaking through a barrier, leaving our past behind. We were out. Everything lay ahead of us. Even though Canada was a few thousand miles away, at least we were headed somewhere. We had a destination. We had a goal. There was some kind of, I don't know, purpose to it. That was more than we ever had back home.

Ten miles into Georgia, we got off the interstate and took smaller, less-traveled roads, ones that showed up as the thinnest lines on our atlas. We figured if the cops were looking for us, they'd watch the interstates and bigger highways. We were trying to disappear into the map. The line Curtis drew was erratic, like a moth tracking a moving light. We took roads that headed north and west with no design beyond what turn to take next.

Late in the afternoon, my eyelids drooped like someone had sewn a five-pound weight to them. I had barely slept the night before, and it was catching up to me. Curtis's eyelids bobbed too. We needed to find some place to stop for the night, a park or some country road that led into the woods, out to nowhere, away from everything. Between all that had happened last night and that day, we were exhausted.

We passed a handmade sign along the side of the road that read: "Come Along, Hound Dog, to the Saturday Gathering. The King Lives in All of Us! 4 PM at Hamilton Park." A few miles later we came across another sign: "Don't Be Cruel! Come and Praise Elvis!" Then another, "It's Now or Never. Turn Here."

It was a little after four. We figured it would still be going on, and the park was exactly what we needed—a place to get some rest, maybe sleep for the night. I turned in.

Tall pine trees lined the entrance. The road sloped upward and flattened at a large parking lot. A group collected at one end. There must've been about fifty people, all gathered around a pavilion with streamers hanging from the roof. All of them faced a guy standing on a picnic table, speaking to them. The guy had bushy sideburns and thick black hair pushed up in a pompadour.

"Holy crap! Is that Elvis?" I asked.

Curtis laughed. The guy did look like Elvis, but you could tell it wasn't, even from a distance. But there was definitely a resemblance. "Could be."

The guy waved his hands in the air, and his head rocked as he spoke. I had no idea what he was talking about, but he was sure excited about it. The people who watched him seemed excited too.

We drove past the group, found an empty pavilion set back in the pine trees, and parked near it. Curtis pulled the gun out from under the seat and put it in his pack. I dragged the cooler out of the

Dart, lugged it up the path to the pavilion, and set it on a table. Curtis followed me, carrying his pack and the bag of groceries.

At times, the voices from the group bubbled with energy, or laughed together at something the Elvis guy said. I wanted to know what he was talking about. I wanted to know what brought them all together like that.

After we made another trip to the car for our sleeping bags and a few other things, Curtis and I went over to the gathering. He was curious too.

The closer we got, the less the guy looked like Elvis. He kept his hair the way Elvis did and had long sideburns. But he had a beak nose, and his face was pockmarked like he used to have acne real bad. He looked old too, maybe in his mid-forties. Of course, that was the same age that Elvis would've been. His shiny leather boots, about two sizes too big for his feet, clomped around on top of the table as he spoke.

There was a wide mix of people gathered in front of him: young couples, old couples, a group of teenage boys, a few families. Some echoed the guy's sentiments; others nodded their heads along with him.

We eased our way into the middle of the group. One lady with her two kids smiled at us as we settled in next to her.

One older guy with a salt-and-pepper beard stood toward the back of the group with his arms folded across his chest, staring intently at the Elvis guy.

A thin woman stood in front, hunched over tensely, clutching something black and shiny to her chest. It appeared to be a doll, but it was hidden beneath her arms. Her eyes were wide and wild.

Curtis nudged me and nodded toward that lady. His expression said, "*Look at that whack job.*"

"The Lord always grants you what you need. That's why he gave us Elvis," the guy said.

The guy with the salt-and-pepper beard said, "Amen." He struck me as being wrapped a little tight too.

"I've spent most of my life on the road." The Elvis guy strutted across the top of the picnic table. "Since I was ten. Takes some getting used to. Being out there on the road. Being alone. A lot of lonely nights. A lot of long drives down Lonely Street." The pitch of his voice rose and fell. "About a year after Elvis died, on one of those long, lonely nights, I had an experience. It changed my life. It was about two in the morning, and I was tired. I probably should've stopped at a hotel, but I had to be in Birmingham that next morning. But I sure was tired. Exhausted." He looked down and shook his head. "But it was more than that." He surveyed the crowd. "There was something missing here." He pointed to his heart. He stood tall on top of a picnic table. On the bench below him, a large leather trunk-style suitcase rested. "It was six months after my daddy died. I wasn't right, in my heart, in my soul. Some days, it was hard for me to keep going on. Some days, I felt like giving up. And that night I wanted to give up. I didn't want to go on. I thought about stopping at a rest area and sleeping for a couple hours, but I kept going. I was fighting off sleep but close to giving in, to falling asleep behind the wheel, when a hitchhiker appeared out of nowhere on the side of the road. Like I said, the Lord gives you what you need, and I needed company. I needed someone to help me stay awake, someone to help me through that night. When I stopped to pick him up, he kept his head down and his collar turned up around his face, so I didn't get a good look at him. It was rainy and cold, so I didn't think anything about it.

"Well, we drove along, sharing each other's company. He was a polite boy with a deep voice. Soothing. I could tell he had a good upbringing and all. He was always saying thank you and please. Calling me sir. We talked about places we'd been and music we liked. All my tiredness, all my weariness, all the ache in my heart left me. I felt reborn. I asked him where he was headed. He said, 'I'm going to Memphis to see my momma. I'm going home.' As we got closer to Memphis, I asked him where exactly he wanted me to drop him. He said anywhere near Elvis Presley Boulevard. When I stopped to let him out, he thanked me. And I asked, 'What's your name, son?' He smiled sheepishly, and in that moment, the light from the inside of the car hit him just right. And I looked hard at him, and when I recognized him, I felt like I had been struck by a thunderbolt. 'My name is Elvis Presley, sir. You have a good night.' I knew right then. It was Elvis. No doubt." He paused. He scanned the audience. Everyone remained quiet, everyone's eyes fixed on him.

The lady holding the doll put her hand to her mouth.

"Elvis lives!" the man with the beard said.

"He's still out there," someone else said.

Curtis snorted out a chuckle. The lady that smiled at us looked at him. I wasn't sure what to believe. The guy sounded sincere, but I didn't know. It was hard to buy that story. I didn't believe Elvis was still alive, and I sure didn't believe in ghosts or anything like that. That crap didn't exist.

"Before I could say another word, he was gone. I sat there for the longest time thinking about what had happened. There was no doubt in my mind that I gave a ride that night to Elvis's spirit, his ghost—or maybe it was him. Some people say, maybe he is still out there somewhere, roaming the country. But whether it was him or his spirit, he helped me through that long night. I took it as a sign, a portent for my purpose in life. To share my story with others who loved Elvis and spread the word. The king lives on."

"I knew it!" The man with the beard said. "He's still with us." He turned, casting his gaze around the group.

"Elvis came back from the dead. It's true." The woman with the doll fell to her knees. She raised one hand above her head, still gripping the doll to her chest with the other. "I have something to say!"

Curtis nudged me. "Here it comes."

She held the doll out for us all to look at. It was Elvis, dressed in black leather and holding a microphone. "I have something to say!"

The crowd became silent. All eyes went to her.

"A week after Elvis died, this doll." She moved the doll through the air to give everyone a good look. "This doll! It came to life on my bureau. It started walking and dancing around. And singing. Oh my god, was it singing." She began prancing the doll in the air. She raised the pitch of her voice to imitate the doll. "I'm a hunka' hunka' burning love. I'm a hunka' hunka' burning love." She pulled the doll back to her chest. "It was a sign. Elvis was talking to me. He's among us." She cast her gaze around the group. "He has never left us. Just like in that song, he is burning love." She stood up and held out the doll to the lady next to her, as if offering up her proof.

"Thank you for sharing your story." The Elvis guy held up his arm. "We all have been touched by Elvis in some way. That's what brought us all here. And that's why I ride around the countryside looking for people like you, like us, so we can share our experiences. We must all keep him alive in our hearts, in our souls. That's what he would want, and if anyone would like to take home a memento or a valued Elvis keepsake?" He reached down and opened his case. He leaned over the contents with a toothy grin. "Please feel free to look through my wares."

There were key rings, statues, buttons, curios, decals, and bumper stickers with Elvis on them. He had necklaces, earrings, big silver belt buckles, bracelets. All kinds of bangles and baubles. There were Elvis-head key rings, glass snow globes with Elvis singing, and a section of sunglasses like Elvis used to wear. It all amounted to a dime-store jewelry department of Elvis paraphernalia. In the top of the case, held in place with a leather strap, lay a gold-plated Bible.

The people surged in around him and began groping at the items inside the case. I eased my way forward with the rest of them. Curtis hung back. Several ladies picked up different items and asked that Elvis guy questions. Others handed him money for their purchases.

I picked up one of the snow globes, shook it, and watched the snowflakes fall around Elvis strumming a guitar.

The Elvis guy looked to me in between making change. "Those globes sell for three dollars a piece, but if you want to order a bulk of a hundred, I can sell them to you for two a piece." He scanned the other people. "I can get you whatever you want. Wholesale. I can also order you an inscribed Bible or any paper or stationery: envelopes, writing paper, greeting cards, you name it."

I held it out for Curtis to see.

"It's all crap," he said. He said it loud too. A couple of people turned and looked at him.

I placed it back in the case.

The guy with the salt-and-pepper beard standing right behind Curtis said, "What do you mean, crap?" He was big, taller than Curtis.

"I mean what I said," Curtis leaned in toward him. "This guy is a shyster. You people are a bunch of rubes."

"You watch who you're calling a rube. I ain't no rube."

Curtis stuck his face up toward the guy. "Elvis's ghost rode with him? Come on. The crazy lady with the doll is more believable than that."

"Who are you calling crazy!" The lady held the doll in front of herself like a shield.

"You should watch what you say, son," the man said.

"Come on. That crap is worthless."

"Hold on there, fellows." Elvis climbed down from the picnic table. He got right in front of Curtis and looked up at him. "You're right there. None of this stuff is valuable. But it all depends on what you put stock in. Everyone should decide that for themselves." He put his foot up on one of the benches and leaned into to it. "I had one lady a few years ago who bought one of those Elvis key rings. She had liver cancer, and, as she lay in her bed dying, she had that key ring on her night stand." People started to line up beside him, holding items they wanted to purchase. "Her husband said she would take it off the nightstand and look at it for hours some days. Just stare at it and smile. So to her it meant something, to her it wasn't crap. It helped her through her cancer to the end."

Curtis broke his gaze from Elvis. He crossed his arms and stepped away from the crowd. The guy with the beard brushed past Curtis and asked, "How much for that Bible?"

The Elvis guy put his hand up. "That Bible is not for sale. My daddy was a preacher. He carried that with him from town to town and preached the Word. When he passed away, that Bible was given to me. In my own way, I carry on for him. I can't preach like my daddy could. But I can speak from my heart." He tapped his chest.

Curtis grabbed me and pulled me away. The crowd continued to chatter and mill about the case. Elvis was busy taking in money, making change, and bargaining with the people.

We went back to our pavilion. Curtis climbed up on one of the picnic tables and lay down. He rested the back of his head on his hands and looked up at the trees. Outside of pointing out the highlights of fishing in Canada and voicing his opinion at the gathering of Elvis fans, he had been quiet all afternoon. The crowd around Elvis slowly dissipated.

"Are you all right?" I asked.

Curtis lifted his head and looked at me. "What a bunch of crap. Can you believe those people?" He sounded mad. "Did you see the lady with the doll? How would you like to sit next to her on a four-hour bus ride?"

"Yeah, I know she was a bit out there. But the Elvis guy. He seemed like he believed what he was saying."

"Man, are you kidding me? I don't believe you. It's a scam. So he can sell that crap in his case. He's a con man preying on those people. I love Elvis too. But come on. That shit don't mean nothing."

I knew Curtis was probably right, but I wondered. Maybe that Elvis guy did believe that he gave a ride to Elvis's ghost. And maybe he was telling those people his honest experience. And whether it happened or not, he believed it, and they sure believed him. I envied them. Envied that they could have that kind of faith in anything. But I couldn't say that to Curtis, not without him going coo-coo for Coco Puffs.

But having that kind of faith was something I wanted to understand because I wanted it too. I wanted something that I could believe in. And why not Elvis? I felt more connected to Elvis than to anything.

For me, the thing that elevated Elvis in my mind was when I heard him sing "Unchained Melody" for the first time. That was the moment that set him apart from the other rock stars. That was the moment when I started to idolize him,

The recording was part of a television special that aired two months after he died. But the song wasn't included in the show. It was released as a separate recording the following year. I'll never forget the first time I listened to it. When Elvis hit that big note, it was perfect. It was beautiful. It was like listening to all the beauty, all the music of the universe surging out from him. It made me believe there was something to this world, something beyond what you could feel with your hands or see with your eyes. There was something we all shared at some innate level. Something that connected us. I wanted to believe that, anyway. And whatever that something was, for that one moment, as I listened to Elvis, I was sure it existed. For that brief instant, in that song, I knew. I was certain. But then it was gone.

I listened to that song over and over trying to find that feeling again, but it was never the same as the first time I heard it. And even with all the other times Curtis and I listened to it, there was a part of me that was always trying to relive that first time, to experience that one perfect moment again. I wanted to know that feeling I had for that all-too-brief instant. But even as bad as I wanted it, part of me knew that I would never have that feeling of complete connectedness again. That it was gone. Forever.

# *Hobo Stew*

If I wasn't so damn hungry, I might have crawled up on a picnic table and gone to sleep, because I was pretty damn tired too. But I hadn't eaten all day, so hunger won out over exhaustion.

But dinner was looking pretty dismal that night. We didn't have any charcoal or even a pot to heat up our can of chili. We didn't even have a can opener. I felt stupid for getting that chili without thinking about a can opener. If we couldn't get into that can, all we had to eat was four cold burritos, potato chips, and a block of cheddar cheese.

That Elvis guy was tearing down the streamers around his pavilion and getting ready to leave. Everyone else had cleared out. I was pretty sure, living on the road like he did, he would have a can opener. He might let us borrow it.

He closed his case, latched it shut, and hefted it off the table. He leaned against the weight of it as he carried it toward a sky-blue pickup truck. The truck was old, like from the fifties, and had rounded wheel wells and a huge hood with a gleaming silver angel at the point. He slid his case across the front seat. He closed the door and stood back with his hands on his hips, and then he went back to the table to get a few more things.

I told Curtis I was going over to ask him about a can opener.

"If not, I'm sure he'd sell you one with an Elvis head on it."

I ignored him.

"That was quite a story," I said as I approached the guy.

He nodded and closed the door of his truck. He took a handkerchief out of his back pocket and wiped the back of his neck with it.

"Would you happen to have a can opener that we could use? We have a can of chili, but we don't have anything to open it with."

"I can accommodate you." He paused and smiled. "I will let you borrow it on one condition."

I looked at him.

"That you fellas break bread with me tonight? I hate eating alone and would appreciate the company."

"I don't know." I knew Curtis wouldn't want the guy joining us. And with us being on the run, I can't say that I could argue with him. It seemed like a risk. "We don't have that much to eat. And we don't have a stove or charcoal either."

"I have some charcoal and some food to add. That's how it is on the road. We all share. I can make some hobo stew."

"Hobo stew?" I asked. "What's that?"

Elvis leaned his head back. "If you've never had it, you owe it to yourself to try it." His eyes lit with excitement. "My, my. It's been months since I've made it. I'll get my stuff together and be right over."

I headed back to our pavilion.

"Did he have a can opener?" Curtis asked.

"Yes."

Curtis studied me. "Where is it?"

"Um, he's bringing it. He's going to join us for dinner."

"What?" Curtis's face snarled. "I don't want that guy coming over here."

I shrugged. It was too late. He was already coming up the path toward us. He carried a small Styrofoam cooler and a wicker suitcase.

He set the cooler on our picnic table and took the lid off. "Let's see what I have in here. Hum, not much. Just a few hot dogs. I do have some charcoal and condiments. And I do have a can opener for that chili."

He opened the wicker case, took out a small bag of briquettes and a can of lighter fluid, and handed them to Curtis. "Why don't you get these started in the grill?"

Curtis looked at me.

I shrugged. "Come on. Just do it."

Curtis went to the grill, dumped in the briquettes, doused them with lighter fluid, then tossed in a match.

Elvis handed me a can opener, and I opened the can of chili. He took four hot dogs, wrapped in torn plastic, out of his cooler and laid them on the picnic table. He pulled out a large black skillet and several plastic plates from his suitcase. He set the skillet on the grill over the flaming coals. His boots huffed as he walked.

"Those boots are cool." I bent over to take a closer look.

"They belonged to my daddy. They're a size too large for me, but I wear them anyway."

Curtis grabbed a couple of beers buried under ice. "Last two." He handed me one. He cracked his open and took a big swallow. I climbed up on one of the picnic tables and sat. I leaned forward with my elbows on my knees. I popped open my beer and took a swig. It tasted good.

"Daddy taught me how to cook hobo stew. When I was a few years younger than you boys, we traveled from place to place in his old Ford pickup. That one right over there. All four of us: me, my daddy, Mom, and Sissy. Lined up across the front seat. Every night, Daddy cooked up hobo stew." He thumped the edge of the pan with the wooden spoon. "Everybody gathered around the fire, contributing whatever they could. The only thing Daddy did better than making stew was preaching. Daddy could make a third-generation atheist see the light. Daddy preached and I sang, while Momma played the organ and my little sister passed around the hat. I love to sing. Always have." He took a small folding knife from his pocket and cut up the hot dogs over the skillet. The slices sizzled as they hit the pan.

"We went to the same towns from year to year. They all knew when we were coming and always greeted us like we were their own."

Curtis walked over to the edge of the pavilion with his back to us. Elvis went on about his family. I could've sat there listening to him all night. He seemed so happy when he talked about his family and what they did and stuff. I enjoyed that. I liked listening to him talk and watching him cook. It helped me forget all the stuff that had happened. The stress of that day eased away from me. I took another sip of beer.

Elvis dumped the chili in with the hissing hot dog chunks. The chili crackled as it hit the hot skillet. He spread it with his spoon. It quenched the sizzling skillet. Steam, thick with the rich, spicy chili smell, rolled into the air. I sucked deeply in through my nose, pulling in as much of the steam as I could. I closed my eyes and let it fill me. The anticipation of the meal consumed me. I took another greedy swallow of my beer.

Elvis went to our cooler and opened it. He took out our burritos and the block of cheddar cheese. He used his knife to cut it all up. He set his knife down on the table and carried the plate of burrito and cheese slices to the grill. He began laying the pieces on top of the bubbling chili. He set the plate down and took up the spoon again.

I watched the cheese slowly melt and the chunks of burrito sink in.

"So did you really see Elvis that night?" I asked. I searched his face for the answer. I wanted to believe that he was telling the truth.

"I think so."

Curtis rolled his eyes. "You know it's bullshit." He bent down and scooped up a handful of twigs out of the dirt. "That didn't really happen."

"Maybe you're right." Elvis nodded and looked down. He reached into his suitcase and took out a couple of tin boxes of spices that he sprinkled over the mix. "I've heard of people that have experienced waking dreams and things like that. And I guess that's possible. I sure was tired that night. But it seemed real to me. But maybe…maybe it didn't happen and I just convinced myself, over time, that it did." He shrugged. "Whatever it was. Now, I choose to believe it. Why else would I tell people about it?"

"Maybe you like selling your baubles. You like taking advantage of people."

"So I do it for the ninety-four dollars I made tonight?" Elvis chuckled. "Hum, I could make more money selling curtain rods door to door."

Curtis got up on the picnic table and sat. He leaned forward, resting his elbows on his knees. He picked through the twigs in his hand, tossing them away one by one. "Maybe you get off by fooling people into believing you."

"Fool people. That would be sad if that were my motivation. A man should try to contribute something positive to this world. We're all brothers. We're all in this together."

Curtis looked at me. "What do you think, Jack?"

My eyes went back and forth between the two of them. "I'd like to believe it. I don't know. It would be nice to believe that Elvis's ghost was out there somewhere roaming around trying to help people."

"Well," Elvis said. "I guess it all comes down to what you choose to believe in this world. A person has to live with those choices and with what they do in their life. Those things stick to you like ink to paper." Elvis put his palms together in the air in front of Curtis.

I shifted in my seat uncomfortably. I felt antsy as hell. I wished we would change the damn subject. Talking about choices and having to live with things. I pictured that old man lying on the ground with blood oozing out of his stomach and his wife kneeling next to him. Both of them looking at us, looking at me. Their eyes burning into me. We had to live with that now. There was no going back. I hoped like hell that old man was doing okay, that he was still alive. "I don't know." I shook my head, trying to shake those thoughts out of my mind.

Curtis considered this for a moment, then shook his head. "Don't mean nothing." He tossed away the rest of the twigs. He got up and stepped away.

Elvis peered down into our bag of groceries and pulled out the potato chips. He opened the bag, took handfuls, and ground them up across the top of the stew. "The stew is finished." Elvis pulled three plates out of his case and spooned the stew onto each plate. He handed one to Curtis, one to me, and kept the last one for himself.

I hung my face over the plate into the wisps of steam that rose from it and took in one last draw of the rich chili and spices. The aroma seemed to flow through me. I pushed my breath out through my nose and dug in. The stew tasted even better than it smelled. I devoured my food. Curtis did the same, and by his expression, I knew he liked it as much as I did.

"So where are you headed?" I scraped the last few drops of chili onto my fork and shoved it into my mouth.

"Every year around this time, I make my way to Graceland for Elvis week." He got up from the picnic table. He took all the dishes, went to a faucet at the edge of the pavilion, and rinsed them off. "I schedule my year around it. I do pretty well there."

"Elvis week?" I asked.

"Ever since Elvis died, during the second week of August, thousands of people of all walks, ways, and means make the pilgrimage to Graceland. I sell a lot of my wares there. But that's not the reason I go. I go to be with people who love Elvis like I do.

"Where are you fellows headed?"

"Canada," Curtis said.

"Canada?" Elvis crinkled his nose. "That's a long way. What are you guys going there for?" He dried the dishes with a towel.

Curtis and I looked at each other. Neither of us was sure what to say. "Ah . . ." I said. "We're brothers. We have an uncle who's going to give us summer jobs as lumberjacks."

Elvis nodded but looked puzzled. "Well, it was nice meeting you fellas. I have to be on my way. I need to make Dawson tonight." He gathered his stuff together and packed it away. "You have a good trip." He grabbed his case and cooler and made his way toward his pickup truck.

"Lumberjacks?" Curtis asked.

"I guess we need to work up a better story."

Elvis got in the truck. The door rang when it closed. He turned the key. The engine groaned but failed to come to life. It sounded like a mechanical dog with a dying battery. He tried again with no luck. He got out, waved to me like "no problem," and opened the hood. He climbed up on the front bumper, his boots slipping off three or four times before he maintained a perch. He immersed himself in the engine and fiddled with it, and then he hopped down and closed the hood that banged heavily into place. He got back in the truck. It rumbled to life, and he drove away.

I unrolled my sleeping bag and laid it on top of a picnic table. Curtis did the same. I took a T-shirt out of my pack and balled it up for a pillow. My jeans whistled against the nylon as I slid into my bag. Night fell, and the glowing red briquettes dimmed beneath the ash deepening around them. The thin, sharp smell of the charcoal rode the air, and I looked up through the pine trees. I wanted to sleep. I sure as hell was tired, but I lay there for what seemed hours.

I was certain Bruce had made it back by now. He would've picked up a ride pretty quick, and then it was only a two-hour drive up 41. I wondered if he had been arrested yet. I doubted that. Probably, he was still waiting for it to come crashing down around him. I didn't think he would fess up. He would cling to the hope that they wouldn't come after him. That he would somehow slip through the cracks. So I figured he was home now and jumping out of his skin every time there was a knock at the door or the phone rang.

What Elvis had said echoed through my mind: "Your choices stick to you like ink to paper." Taking off, running like we did, was delaying the inevitable. The longer we stayed out here and the farther we went, the harder it would be when we went back. Unless we did like Curtis wanted: got to Canada and disappeared into the wilderness. But even if we did make it to Canada, it sure as hell wouldn't be anything like the picture Curtis was painting. Nowhere near.

"What kind of person am I?" Curtis asked. He sounded timid,

afraid, like the darkness had broken down that wall he always put up.

"What do you mean?"

"I was ready to kill those people back there."

"You were scared. And you didn't."

"You stopped me."

"You wouldn't have done it anyway."

"I shot that old man."

I propped myself up and looked over toward Curtis. I could barely make out his form on the picnic table next to me. "That was an accident."

"He's probably dead now."

"We don't know that."

"He was right." Curtis flopped back flat on the table.

"Who?"

"You name it."

No one had ever given Curtis a chance. Not his father. Not any teacher or coach at school. Not anyone. He was marked. He had nothing. I wanted to help him, but I didn't know how. And Curtis could make fun of those Elvis people all he wanted, but at least they had something. What did we have? I had Curtis and he had me and we had Canada. That was it.

I lay there for hours that night with all the events from the day streaming through my head: the shooting, the escape, the drive, the reality that home now was off-limits. It might as well have been surrounded by barbed wire, armed guards, and loose German Shepherds that answered to names like "Killer" and "Fritz." There was no easy way back. Even though I complained about it all the time and bitched about how it sucked, it was now gone from me. Even if we faced up to what happened, it wouldn't be the same. Not really. Not the way it was before we left. I felt so alone. So lost. So small.

I gazed up at the tall pines leaning over me and the stars burning above: blazing beacons reaching out through all the coldness and darkness of space like tiny diamonds set in tar. They winked in the gaps amid the branches and speckled the openings between the tree-tops. They appeared so close to each other but were millions of miles apart, and even farther from me. But I couldn't help but think that something held them all in place, held us all in place. Bound us together. I tasted the burning charcoal in my nose and felt the slow, warm breeze rinse over me while I watched those distinct points of light that began their journeys thousands of years ago and traveled hundreds of millions of miles to me. I couldn't help but wonder, but *hope*, that maybe somehow, in some small, small way, I was a significant part of it all.

# Elvis Plays

I look up at a huge Ping-Pong table. Elvis stands at one end playing against a pulsating cloud of light. The ball clicks and clops off the table and paddles, back and forth, back and forth.

Elvis is young, wearing a pair of pink pants with black stripes down the side and a black silk shirt. He dances around on his side of the table, posing and smiling in between amazing shots. The cloud of light moves its paddle with ease and precision, returning everything, placing the ball at steeper angles and with harder and harder shots. But Elvis gets them all. He moves in a blur to the path of the ball, freezes for an instant, hits, then moves back to the center of the table. Then he's off again, from one side of the table to the other. Sometimes, he does leaps or karate kicks.

The cloud of light hits a hard smash at Elvis. Elvis does a spin and backhand-slaps the ball back over the net. The cloud smashes the ball hard off the table. It soars over Elvis's head. Elvis runs to get it. He dives into space, stretching out his arm and paddle for it.

"Get it, Elvis!" I scream.

"Huh?" He turns to me, and the ball falls to the ground. He

climbs to his feet, glaring, his lip in a snarl. "What are you looking for, Jack?" He brushes off his pants.

"I'm not looking for anything."

"Yeah." Elvis cocks an eyebrow. "If you say so." He chuckles, picks up the ball, and shuffles back to the table. He smiles. "Maybe a better question is: what's looking for you?"

I look down.

Elvis holds the ball to the paddle, preparing to serve. "So that's 10,548,766 to 0."

"You've never scored?" I ask.

Elvis stops in mid-swing and looks at me in disgust. "Score? How the hell am I going to do that, Jack? Don't you think God knows where I'm going to hit the ball? But that's not important, I have something to tell you. You need to look for me."

"Look for you?"

"Yeah, I'm out there somewhere."

"Where?"

He shrugs. "I don't know. You have to figure that out. But I'm telling you to do this. I'm giving you this . . ." He pauses, trying to come up with the right word. "Quest. But I'm out there. And you need to find me. For your sake. For your friend's sake."

"Why?"

"Why?" He leans back. "Did Noah ask why when God told him to build the ark?"

"Yes."

"Well, did God tell him?"

I thought for a minute. "I believe that He did."

Elvis slaps his paddle down on the table and throws up his hands. "I don't claim to have all the damn answers! But I'm telling you—"

The cloud of light darkens and grumbles impatiently.

Elvis puts up his hand. "Just a minute, Father."

I look at Elvis.

"We're all God's children, Jack. But look . . ." Elvis takes a deep breath and places both hands on the table. "Some things I know and some things I don't. But listen to me. Find me. You won't be sorry. And I'm out there. Believe me, I'm out there. It's up to you to find me. And if you do, you may help yourself. You may find some answers." He points at me with his paddle. "And you may help your friend too."

"But how am I going to find you?"

"Figure it out, Jack. You're a smart guy." He raises his eyebrows. "Sort of. Worry about that later. Right now you've got bigger problems. You've got a cop that's about to be all over your ass. So you better wake up."

# *Night Visitor*

I sat up on the picnic table. Light sprayed through the trees around us as a car circled the parking lot. It ground to a stop behind the Dart. The silhouette of police rollers stood on top.

The door creaked as the cop got out with a flashlight. He crouched behind Curtis's car, writing down the license plate number, then went back to his car. He stood in the open door, set his flashlight on the roof, and stretched the radio microphone out of the vehicle. I strained to make out what he said, but I couldn't. I was sure he was having our plate checked.

I didn't see any way out of this. Once he heard back on his radio, we would be hauled away and shipped back to Tampa. Our short life on the run was over. It was almost a relief. "Curtis," I hissed in as loud a whisper as I dared.

Curtis groaned and flopped toward me. "What?"

"A cop."

Curtis lifted himself up to look. "Shit." He got off the picnic table and went to his pack. I heard him rummage through it. In the darkness, I couldn't see what he was doing, but I saw his silhouette shove something under his belt behind his back. He pulled his shirt over it. It had to be the gun. Curtis climbed up onto the picnic table and slid into his sleeping bag.

A knot formed in my gut. "What are you doing?" I hissed.

He didn't say anything.

"Curtis?"

"Shut up. He'll hear us."

The cop put the radio microphone away and closed the door. He adjusted his belt with both hands, grabbed his flashlight, and walked toward us. His free hand swung wide around his belt. He stopped on the path and scanned the pavilion with his light. It paused on me.

He came on toward us. He was too close now for me to say anything to Curtis without him hearing. I sat up on the picnic table. I twisted my legs out of my sleeping bag and looked over at Curtis's form on the picnic table next to me. My body was tense; my jaws clamped together. I wished like hell Curtis hadn't gotten that gun out of his pack.

The cop entered the clearing. He shined his light across Curtis, who pretended to sleep.

He pointed the light at my face. "Good evening," he said. "Kind of late for a picnic. Don't you think?"

The light bit my eyes and I cringed, putting one hand up as a shield.

"Go wake your friend over there."

I went to Curtis and grabbed his shoulder, pulling him onto his back. "Get up, man."

Groaning, Curtis rolled himself to a sitting position. He rubbed the back of his head, like he was waking up.

"What are you boys doing so far from home?" The cop blasted the light into Curtis's face. Curtis recoiled from it.

"We're taking a little camping trip, sir," I said.

"Well, this isn't a camp-ground. I'll give you five minutes to get your stuff together and bring it out to your car."

"What are you arresting us for?" I asked.

The cop directed his light back at me. "I'll ask the questions, son."

Curtis and I stuffed everything into our packs, and we slung our sleeping bags over our shoulders. Curtis's sleeping bag hung down over his back. I grabbed the cooler. The cop walked at our heels. I walked a step behind Curtis. I kept a close eye on him. I put the cooler on the back seat. Everything else we dumped into the trunk. The cop shined his light around the inside of it. I guess he wanted to make sure we didn't have a pound of pot or a dead body back there.

"I want to see your license and registration," he said.

My hand shook as I handed him my license.

"Calm down, son. Everything will be all right." He smiled. A nametag that read *Jacobs* sat below his badge on his chest. His forearm sported a tattoo of an eagle with *Semper Fi* etched underneath.

Curtis opened the passenger side door and reached toward the glove box.

The cop stepped toward him. "What're you doing?"

"My wallet's in there. And the car registration," Curtis said.

"You go slow."

Curtis pushed the button on the glove box, and the door dropped open. Curtis pointed to his wallet. "See?" He handed over his license and registration.

Curtis leaned back against the front end of his car. He slumped like he wanted to fall back asleep, like that was the only thing on his mind.

I stood next to the car. "I'm sorry, sir. I know we shouldn't have been sleeping out here, but we were trying to save our money by not staying in a hotel."

The cop slid our licenses side by side under the clip of his metal board and studied them. "There's a campground five miles down the road." He lifted his head and looked at me. "You're underage."

"Yes sir. I'll be eighteen next month."

He looked to Curtis. "And you just turned eighteen. What are you doing out by yourselves? Do your parents know where you are?"

"Yes."

"This is county land, and you boys are trespassing. Can you give me one reason I shouldn't haul you in?" He wrote down our license numbers.

"Well, sir," I said. "My friend Curtis is going off to the Marines in a couple weeks. We've been friends all through high school, and we've always talked about going hiking in the Smokey Mountains. We've been planning this for months. This is our last chance before he leaves."

The cop stared at our licenses and then paused looking at me, as if he were trying to make a decision about us. Curtis lifted himself off the car and put his hand on his hip. I knew he was positioning it so he could grab that pistol if he needed to. Part of me wanted to scream and ask Curtis what the hell he was thinking; another part of me wanted to warn the cop to watch out. The cop stood there. He kept his gaze on me. He tapped the end of his pen on the metal clipboard. Curtis's lips were clenched, waiting for the cop to make a move, waiting for him to try to arrest us.

"I tell you what. I've already called in your license plate number. If that comes back clean, I'll let you go."

Curtis relaxed and dropped his hand to his side.

"Thank you." I still felt doomed. I was sure that old lady had given the cops our license plate number. And I was sure all the cops in the southeast were looking for us. We were caught dead to rights.

I stared at Curtis, trying to get his attention. He wouldn't look me in the eye.

I moved over next to him. I knew Curtis was going to try something if the cop tried to arrest us. When Curtis went for the gun, I could jump on him and knock him down, knock the gun out of his hand before he could do anything. Or maybe I could step in between him and the cop. Curtis wouldn't shoot me. But what would the cop do if he saw Curtis had pulled a gun? That might get Curtis shot or get *me* shot. But no matter what, I would do something. I couldn't let him take it any further. I had to be ready to stop him.

The radio barked. The cop walked over and picked up the microphone. I glared at Curtis. His eyes narrowed, and he gritted his teeth. He eased his hand back onto his hip.

"Go ahead," the cop said. The reply came. It was garbled and full of static. I couldn't make out a thing. With his hand resting on the butt of his gun, the cop headed back toward us. The cop's boots scuffed the asphalt as he walked up to me. Curtis edged forward, his eyes getting wider; he began inching his hand behind him. I took a small step to the side to position myself better. I leaned forward, setting my weight to dive at Curtis. I bent my knees slightly, getting ready to spring if I had to.

"You boys can go." He handed me back my license. My shoulders slumped. I felt a breath of air leave me. "I told you there was nothing to be scared of."

He walked over to Curtis and handed him his license.

I chuckled nervously.

"Get the hell out of here, and I don't want to hear about you again tonight."

We got in the car and took off, Curtis behind the wheel. The cop followed us out of the park. After we pulled onto the highway, Curtis rolled his window down and air blasted through the car. "Well, you got us out of that one." Curtis took the gun out from behind his back and put it back under my seat. "The Marines thing. That was good."

I didn't say anything. I sat there, squeezing the armrest as hard as I could, digging my fingernails into it. "What the hell were you doing?" I stared straight ahead. I didn't even want to look at him.

"What do you mean?"

"Were you going to take out that gun or what?"

"I don't know. All I know is nobody is taking me back. I told you that."

"What would you have done if he tried to arrest us? You sure as shit weren't going to shoot him."

He paused then shrugged. "I could've cuffed him up in the back of his car, and we could've left him there. Come on. Nothing happened. We got out of it. You should be happy."

I shook my head. I was sure the cop was going to haul us in, that our license plate would've been flagged, that they would've been looking for us by now. Maybe that old man wrote it down wrong. Maybe that kind of information wasn't shared between the Florida and Georgia police, or it took time. I tried to tell myself that they weren't after us, but I knew that wasn't right. We were just lucky. It would catch up with us eventually. It had.

I crunched the magazine cover with my heel, jamming it underneath the passenger seat as far as I could. Before this, I thought that episode with the old man was an isolated incident, that nothing like that could happen again. I was stupid to think that. Especially given what happened in that store and Curtis's mental state over the last few months. I was throwing my life away. Not that Curtis had given me much choice. How long could I stay with him if he was bent on self-destruction and if all he was going to do was take me down with him? I took the gun out from under the seat. I held it in both my hands and stared at it. The car went across a short bridge over a river.

"What are you doing?"

I threw the gun out the window and watched it twirl out of sight over the rail.

"What the fuck!" Curtis put his foot on the brake and looked back like he was thinking about going back and looking for it. *Good luck finding it in the river,* I thought. He faced forward and stomped his foot on the gas. "What'd you do that for?" Curtis asked.

"Why do you think?" I rested my elbow on the door. The wind flapped the cuff of my T-shirt.

"You dumbass."

"That's twice I thought you were going to do something crazy."

Curtis didn't say anything. He just glared ahead at the road.

He was pissed at me, but I didn't care because I sure as hell was pissed at him. I turned and looked out my window. We went on like that for hours. We didn't say one word to each other.

As the night deepened into the morning, my eyes kept dropping shut, and I kept fighting it. I never felt so tired in my whole life. We hadn't slept at all the last two days. I would've given anything for a nice bed to sleep in or some place to take a shower. Neither of us was really in the mood to talk about our options. So we kept going. We had to. What else could we do? We sure as hell weren't going to try parking somewhere on the side of the road and sleeping. Not again. I was sure we could've found some cheap fleabag to crash at, but that would've been the end of our cash.

I didn't know how Curtis kept going, and I wasn't about to ask him, but he must've been as tired as I was. The only thing keeping me awake was how pissed off I was. That must've been the only thing that kept him going too, because every time I snuck a glance over at him, his gaze was fixed, burning straight ahead at the road in front of him. The whole time I didn't say a damn word to Curtis; I didn't want to lose the war of silence between us. I didn't want to give him that. So we kept going, headed nowhere, but at least Curtis was driving fast.

We broke into Alabama around five that morning. Ghosts of mist glided across the road as morning light seeped up from the ground. It felt strange, like we had driven into some kind of a dreamscape.

Curtis leaned forward and glared into the thin mist ahead of us. A man emerged from it. He stood on the shoulder of the road. Curtis slowed down. The guy started jumping around, waving a cardboard sign. Something was written on it, but I couldn't make it out.

"What the hell is that?" I asked.

"I don't know." These were the first words Curtis and I had spoken since I threw the gun out the window.

The guy held up his hands for us to stop and stepped into the road. A large duffel bag was slung over his shoulder. He put his hands together as if pleading us, and then he held the sign steady. I was able to read it, one word written in heavy black charcoal: "Nirvana."

# *Nirvana*

The guy took a step into our lane. Given Curtis's state of mind, I wasn't sure that was the smartest thing for him to do. The sign bent in his grasp as he put both hands out like he was planning to stop the car himself.

Curtis put his foot on the brake. He eased around the guy and pulled to the side of the road. The red taillights glowed up behind us. "Let's see what he wants."

The guy jogged up to us. He put one hand on the roof of the car and grabbed for the door handle.

"Hold on!" Curtis planted his elbow on his door and twisted to look at him. "Not so fast."

The guy took his hand off the door and shrugged. "I just need a lift, man." The green canvas duffel bag slid down his shoulder into his other hand. "Come on, friend. It's not far. You're headed that way."

Curtis rolled his eyes over at me.

"Where are you going?" I wobbled my head in a shake, about to tell him to beat it. I wasn't sure why Curtis stopped in the first place.

Maybe he wondered where Nirvana was.

"Didn't you read my sign?" He held it out for me. The lettering was like calligraphy.

"Yeah," I said. "Not sure we can get you there."

"I'm kidding. I live real close. Just down this road."

"Look, we really don't have time for this, and we don't know you. So—"

Curtis took his foot off the brake; the car started to drift forward.

"Hold on! Hold on!" The guy gripped the top of Curtis's door. "You guys look as tired as I feel, and you smell like you've been living in the swamp for a week."

Curtis narrowed his eyes at him. "So?"

"So if you give me a lift, I'll let you crash at my place. You can clean up."

I looked to Curtis. We sure needed some sleep, and the guy was right about how we smelled.

"Come on. You're the first car that's come by in half an hour. Help me out." He was only a year or two older than us and looked like any kid from school. He sure didn't strike me as someone who would call the cops. And with the cold vibe that existed between Curtis and me right then, anything that broke the silence would be welcome.

I raised my eyebrows to Curtis: *What do you think?* His sagging eyes gave me my answer. "Okay, get in."

"Cool." The guy opened the back door and flopped onto the back seat. He slung his bag down heavily next to him. He wore faded jeans torn out at the knee.

"Well, where is Nirvana?" I asked.

"It's anywhere you want it to be, man." He laughed and pointed up the road. "Ten miles up the road."

Curtis pulled ahead.

"I'm Skeeter." He flicked his long, wavy red hair over his shoulder and rubbed his finger over a small mole on his cheek.

"I'm Jack, and this is Curtis." I extended my hand back for him to shake. "What are you doing out here this time of morning?"

"My bud ditched me last night. I've been hiking home ever since. Not many people cruise this highway this time of the morning, and if they do, they sure aren't looking to give any scruffy-hippy-looking dudes a ride." He chuckled. "I was getting desperate. That's why I made my sign. What are you guys up to?"

Curtis eyed Skeeter in the rearview mirror. "Just out for a ride."

"Out for a ride? Really?" Skeeter looked out his side window and nodded. "Okay. If you say so. At five in the AM. Driving through God-knows-where, Alabama."

"We're taking a trip up into the mountains. Camping. We don't have the cash for a hotel," I said.

Skeeter bounced to the center of the back seat and leaned forward. He stuck his head up between Curtis and me. "Do you need cash?"

"We're all right," Curtis said.

"Okay. Like I said, you guys are welcome to crash at my place. And if you are strapped for cash, I might be able to help you out there too."

"How so?" I asked.

"We'll talk later." Skeeter patted his bag with his hand. "But I owe you guys. I pay my debts."

I glanced at the fuel gauge: less than a quarter tank. We had about thirty bucks left. We didn't have enough money to get out of Alabama. I didn't know what we were going to do for food either. We didn't have many options. But something didn't feel right about Skeeter's offer. It felt shady. We didn't need any more trouble.

Skeeter directed us onto a long dirt road driveway that ended at a trailer. Next to the trailer was a brown Chevy Impala. Car metal curled down around the empty rim of the front wheel. The driver's side headlight was busted out. Beside the trailer stood an oak tree with a big piece of bark knocked out of it.

"I ran into that tree last week. My cigarette fell out of my mouth and started burning my crotch. Almost cracked my skull." Skeeter rubbed the back of his head as if recalling the incident. "Tomorrow, I'll call a tow truck or something and get it taken care of."

Curtis parked the car in front of the trailer. We went in. An answering machine sat on the counter of the kitchen. Skeeter hit the play button. There were about fifteen messages on it. Most were people asking if they could come over or asking what was going on.

"You guys can rack out on the couch or on the floor. I need to crash too." He went to the telephone and turned the ringer off. He went into the other room with his bag and shut the door.

I got my sleeping bag out of the trunk, spread it on the floor, and lay on top of it. Things were still frigid between Curtis and me. We didn't say two words to each other. And any time either of us got close to looking the other in the eye, the other was repelled like we were the opposite ends of two magnets. Maybe things would look better after we got some sleep. Maybe we would be able to stand each other again. Maybe if I got some rest, I could figure out what we should do. Or what I should do. I couldn't get past the fact that Curtis was ready to pull a gun on a cop. Bruce was starting to look like the smart one. I wondered if I should head back. Leave Curtis to go on alone. I wasn't sure how I could do anything for him by staying with him anyway. He sure didn't listen to me.

I wanted to help him, but how? He was set on a path, a path that only had one end, and for him there was no turning back. How long could I stick with him without dooming myself? Without him dragging me down with him?

I kept thinking about that dream I had too. Elvis had seemed so real. But how could it be? I told myself it was brought on by a combination of that chili I ate, all the crap that happened, and listening to that Elvis guy. It was me telling myself what I wanted most to hear, giving myself what I most wanted: some purpose, some place to go, some place that wasn't Canada. But there was no way I could track down Elvis. That made no sense. He was dead and that was that. That religious peddler may have believed that he had seen Elvis or

Elvis's ghost, but I sure as hell wasn't convinced. And it was going to take a lot more than a dream to convince me.

But Elvis did tell me about the cop. I had read somewhere that sometimes people will pull things they hear into their dreams. Like if you hear a train going by in the distance, that train will become part of your dream. Maybe I heard the car driving into the parking lot when I was sleeping, and I added that. At that time of night, the chances were anyone coming into that lot would be a cop or a security guard. That made the most sense, a lot more sense than the ghost of Elvis popping into my head to warn me.

Curtis got cozy on the couch and pulled a blanket over himself. I slid into my sleeping bag. It didn't take long before sleep descended on me, and it was like a three-hundred-pound lady dropping onto a barstool.

•••••••••••

I woke up to someone pounding on the door. I had no idea what time it was, or day for that matter. I could've been asleep for two or three days for all I knew. Curtis groaned himself awake on the couch. Skeeter popped out of his bedroom and went to the door. "Who is it?" he asked.

"It's me, man."

"Minnow." Skeeter smiled at us. He opened the door.

Light invaded the room. It hurt my eyes, it was so bright. I gazed up at a skinny, pale guy with stringy, dark hair. He had thick, dark-rimmed glasses and seemed jittery too, like he had just downed a two-liter Mountain Dew.

He looked at me and then at Curtis, who was sitting on the couch. "Who are these guys?"

"Jack and Curtis. They picked me up last night." He looked hard at Minnow. "Which is more than you can say."

"I had some car trouble." Minnow bobbed his head up and down sheepishly.

I took that as my cue. "It's time we got on our way." I climbed to my feet. Curtis got up from the couch.

"What's your rush?" Skeeter put his hand on my shoulder and eased me back down. "I told you I have a business opportunity."

"What would that be?"

"We've carved ourselves out our own niche in the pot dealing world. Our motto is: 'We deliver too.' For a minimal charge, five dollars per delivery, we have a doorstep service. Since my car is out of commission, you guys can take that part of the business and pocket the delivery charge yourselves."

"I don't know," I said.

"Come on. You'd be doing me a favor. And it's easy money."

Minnow gave Skeeter a funny look.

"Don't worry," Skeeter said. "They're okay."

"So I guess you were successful then. How'd it go?"

"Smooth as glass. Until you didn't show up. It's good stuff too. We'll be able to turn this over in no time."

I didn't like it. We didn't need to get involved with dealing drugs. We were in enough trouble already. It was a risk we didn't need to take. "We need to get going."

"Come on. You'd be doing me a favor. It'll only be until I can get my car fixed. Just a couple days."

"We sure could use the cash," Curtis said. He looked to me. "We don't have enough cash to get out of Alabama?"

"It's not a good idea."

"Why don't you guys talk about this between yourselves?" Skeeter reached over to the phone and turned the ringer on. "As of now, we're open for business. We must adjourn to my room and prepare for our patrons." Skeeter grabbed a box of Baggies out of the kitchen. He and Minnow went into his bedroom and shut the door.

Curtis planted his feet on the floor and leaned forward. "How are we going to get anywhere without cash? If we stay here for a week, we could make enough to get us pretty far. Maybe even all the way to Canada."

I shook my head. "What if we get busted?"

"What does one more thing matter?"

I felt everything crushing down around me. I felt like I was sinking in deeper and deeper.

"It's either this or give up, and you know that. Come on. Let's give it a chance."

I knew Curtis was right. To keep going, we needed cash. And chances of finding ways to make money on the road were about zero. And it might be good for us to stay off the highways for a few days, to lay low. Maybe hiding out was the right thing for us. It was a risk. But wasn't anything we did a risk? And it would give me time to think about everything and decide whether I should head back home or keep going. I knew the smart thing would be to head back. But maybe I could convince Curtis to come with me or to turn himself in. Maybe after a couple of days of thinking about it, that might sound better to Curtis. I couldn't help but think that ultimately, that was his best option too. "Okay. I guess we don't have a choice."

We went to the bedroom door and knocked.

"Come in," Skeeter said.

A large brick of pot lay on top of a garbage bag on the floor. Wearing a pair of gold spectacles with small, square frames, Skeeter sat at a table in front of a set of scales. Thin strands of hemp coiled across the table like dried spiderwebs. He pried off a large chunk from the brick like he was pulling apart a pad of steel wool. The hemp, intertwined within the buds and leaves, stretched out and snapped strand by strand. He set the chunk on the table and started breaking it down further.

"So what's the word?" Skeeter glanced at Curtis over his spectacles. He looked like an accountant, or a banker, almost. He threw loose strands of hemp onto the table.

Skeeter dropped a small handful of pot onto one of the scales' pallets, which shifted down slightly. He eyed the scales, then added some more.

"We're your guys," Curtis said.

"You guys won't be sorry. Like I said, it's easy money." Satisfied by the balance, Skeeter brushed the pot off the pallet and into a Baggie and rolled it up. He tossed it onto a pile of rolledup Baggies. "Great! Let's have a couple of celebratory bong hits." He grabbed a bud of pot and led us into the living room. Curtis and I had smoked weed every so often. We never looked to score any but didn't turn it down either.

Skeeter pulled a tall bong out from behind his couch and filled the bowl. Minnow shuffled to the stereo sitting on a peach crate underneath the window and put on an album: *Animals* by Pink Floyd. Skeeter handed the bong and lighter to Curtis. He took a big hit. A series of coughs exploded from him. He coughed so hard tears rolled down his face. He passed the empty bong back to Skeeter.

Skeeter laughed. "Pretty good stuff, huh." Skeeter filled the bowl and handed it to me.

I looked at it. I knew I shouldn't, but everything was pressing down on me. I had this knot in my gut the size of a coconut. I felt I was on the verge of some kind of a breakdown. Maybe a couple hits would do me some good, buy some distance from all the stuff rumbling through my head. Help me take a break from thinking about everything, to escape it, for a while anyway. I took the bong from Skeeter.

I put it to my mouth. Skeeter held the lighter over the bowl, and I inhaled. Smoke filled the tube and drained into me. It burned my throat. I took my finger off the hole and sucked out the remaining smoke. I coughed almost as hard as Curtis had. The bong went around one more time, everyone taking a turn.

I leaned back on the couch and gazed around the room as the weed leaked through my head. A guitar growled and woofed, imitating a barking dog. I noticed myself breathing and watched my chest rise and fall. I became afraid, like I was doing something wrong, but I had no idea what that something was.

I noticed the clock on the wall had no hands.

"What time is it?" I asked.

"It's daytime," Minnow said.

Curtis laughed.

Several drawings with Skeeter's name in the lower corner hung on the walls around the room. Above the couch was a charcoal sketch of a beautiful girl. She had long hair that curled down her front around her perfectly shaped breasts. An electric organ undulated through the room. A drawing of a wizard that looked like Gandalf from *Lord of the Rings* was on the wall, next to that a painting of a butterfly stretching out of its chrysalis. The butterfly's head was tilted back looking up. Its tongue coiled in front of its face. Huge, delicate wings, painted bright like a stained-glass window, were unfolding. I couldn't take my eyes off of it.

"That's awesome." A smile eased across my face.

"I call that Butterfly Dude," Skeeter said.

Minnow laughed hysterically. He sat cross-legged in the middle of the floor and rocked back and forth, stretching his faded blue T-shirt around his kneecaps.

I rested against the soft cushions of Skeeter's couch. I didn't feel scared. I didn't feel restless. I felt removed from what we had done, like all the crap that had happened was somehow far away from where we were now, like it was all part of some bizarre dream that never happened. That was very soothing to me. It seemed that staying was the right decision. The album ended. The needle of the record player scratched and bumped against the record label with a steady rhythm. I looked at the clock on the wall, and somehow, the thumping of the needle made it seem as if the clock was marking time forward.

# *Burnt*

The next few days melted together into a jumble of bong hits, burning candles, and a stream of blurry people drifting in and out. We got stoned when we woke up. We got stoned when people came by. In between getting stoned, we made deliveries to houses where we got stoned. Whenever we got back from a delivery, there would be a new group of people sitting around Skeeter's mobile home getting stoned. That went on till early in the morning every night. Then we got up the next afternoon, got stoned, and started all over again.

Skeeter was right about the money. It rolled in. The phone rang every fifteen or twenty minutes. Minnow or Skeeter wrote down the names of the people who wanted deliveries. Whenever there were ten or more people on the list, Curtis and I made a run. All the deliveries were in the town of Dugan, a couple miles away.

We made about thirty deliveries the first night. Minnow went with us to show us around and make sure we didn't take off with the pot and the money.

At one stop, a guy asked Minnow, "So what happened with the cops the other night?"

"Huh?" Minnow's eyes bugged open.

"The cops. The other night. They had you lit up."

"Oh, they pulled me over for speeding just to hassle me."

"I guess they were hassling you. I thought they were hauling you in, man."

Minnow grinned and nodded. "It wasn't anything."

When we got back in the car, Curtis asked him, "What was that all about?"

"Oh, nothing."

"Why didn't you mention that to Skeeter?" I asked.

"That happened like a month ago. That guy was wasted, man. He doesn't remember. It was no big deal."

When all the weed had been sold, except Skeeter's private stash, Curtis and I had pockets stuffed with fives, tens, and twenties.

The morning after our last round of deliveries, I woke up on the floor of Skeeter's living room. Skeeter had a sketchpad propped up on his knees and was drawing a picture of Curtis who sat next to him on the couch. Minnow lay on the floor with his head propped up on a partially deflated basketball.

I rolled to my side and pushed myself up. I rubbed what felt like clods of strawberry jam out of my eyes. My head felt like television static was blasting through it. "What day is it anyway? Is it Tuesday?"

"Man, it's Thursday." Skeeter scratched his charcoal against the paper. He laughed. "Welcome to Nirvana."

"No, man, it's Friday," Minnow said.

Skeeter shrugged. "What's the difference? It's one of the later days of the week, anyway."

They both laughed.

We had been gone over a week. I thought about Mom, and I was hit with a wave of guilt. She must be going nuts with me vanishing like I had, especially since she probably knew the whole acid story of what happened, or at least whatever version of the truth Bruce was sharing with everyone.

But I felt bad about my mom. That last year, I came and went as I pleased. I guess a lot of that was because I was so damn restless. That was one of the benefits of being at Skeeter's—I never felt restless. Between the joints and the bong hits, I never felt anything, really.

But at home, being restless was a constant condition. I don't know why I got like that. I wasn't always that way. Restlessness crept up on me as I got older. When I was a kid, I didn't feel that way. We had this antique clock on the shelf by the front door. The clock belonged to my grandmother and needed winding a couple times a week. It made a slight metallic clink with each second and a tinny chime clanged every half hour. I used to love listening to it. I would lie on the floor in the morning and listen to the minutes slowly tick away. I could do that for hours. But now. Now, I couldn't stand it. Hearing it made me feel like a hyper dog with a wild hair up its ass.

But here with Skeeter, the clock on the wall had no hands. There was something attractive about that, especially since we were running from the law and, potentially, a murder charge—something very attractive. But we couldn't do it forever.

"We ought to get back out on the road." I looked at Curtis.

He nodded.

"What's your hurry? Just hang." Skeeter picked a joint up off the table and lit it. "I should hear from my guy shortly, and we'll be back in business." He handed it to Minnow. "What are you going to do in Canada anyway?" Skeeter asked.

We had told them about heading to Canada. We didn't tell them about the shooting or the cops being after us. We said we were brothers, and we were sick of things back home because of Mom's new asshole boyfriend.

Curtis took a hit and looked at the joint, pondering what Skeeter had said. He turned to me. "Maybe we should stay a while longer."

"Yeah, just chill," Minnow said.

"We've chilled enough," I said. "I'm getting burnt out. We could stay here for two years and still being doing the same shit we're doing now—getting up, getting stoned, and watching TV reruns all day long."

"What's wrong with that?" Skeeter looked at me. "We enjoy. And for us it's about friendship. All the people we sell to, they're like family. They would do anything for us. And Minnow and me, I've known him since the second grade. I'd give my life for him."

Minnow nodded. He held his fist up in the air toward Skeeter. "To the end, bro."

Skeeter nodded. "To the end." He put his fist up. "This is like a community. We're offering you the chance to stay for a while. See if you like it. Try it out." Skeeter picked up his pad.

Curtis held out the joint to me. I looked at it, telling myself to pass on it, telling myself I needed to get my head clear again. But I took the joint and a hit, then handed it to Minnow.

"We can leave tomorrow," Curtis said.

The weed seeped into my head. "That sounds good." I nodded.

That morning scene was replayed for the next couple of days. We would get up and talk about leaving. Skeeter would pass around a joint. In a couple hours, we decided it was too late to leave or too much effort, and we started talking about leaving tomorrow.

I came to learn that tomorrow was the day Skeeter did most everything he was going to do. Every day, after we said we would get on the road in a little bit, he said, "Yeah, I need to get motivated and get my car towed to the shop," or, "Yeah, I ought to get out there and fire up that lawn mower and mow the grass." In a couple hours Skeeter would say, "I'll do it tomorrow."

As the days went by it ate at me, but I still didn't push too hard to leave. Mostly because I had decided that when we did leave I would head back home. I could only see one end for us on the road. And that was an end that was not good for Curtis or for me.

I couldn't take it any further. Even though I felt like I was abandoning Curtis, I couldn't let him drag me down. And after that episode with the cop, I didn't think that Curtis would draw the line at anything. And I wasn't sure what I could do to stop him if we got into anything like that again. When we left, I planned to have him drop me at a bus station, and I would take a Greyhound home.

But I felt crappy as hell about it. I knew I needed to talk to Curtis, to tell him my plans. I wasn't looking forward to that. Nobody ever gave Curtis a chance. Back in the 10th grade, Curtis, Bruce, and I took biology together. We had a big project that was due at the end of the year. Bruce got straight A's in everything. He was the golden boy. All the teachers loved him. I floated by with B's and C's, and Curtis floundered with grades a little lower than mine.

The biology teacher, Mr. Crab, had it in for Curtis from day one. All the teachers did, really; it was like Curtis bore a mark that they all could see. But Curtis liked biology. It was the one class where he always read the text and actually talked in class, even though most of the time he was arguing with something Crab said. Curtis got a B for the first half of the year, a landmark grade for him.

Curtis did better the second half of the year. He busted his ass on the final project. It was on honeybees. It was a lot better than mine. Curtis did an awesome model of a honeybee. I did some stupid thing on the moon. It wasn't much, but good enough for a C. But Curtis's project was better than anyone else's. It was a lot better than Bruce's. He did some shitty-ass project on the affect of erosion on mountains. I mean, we lived in Florida. We didn't have any mountains. He bragged about how he had made all his data up. And how he got through all his classes through bullshit and ass-kissing.

When grades were handed out, Bruce got an A and Curtis got a B. Curtis went on about how he didn't give a shit one way or another. But I knew that was bullshit. I tried to talk him into entering his project into the science fair. But he wouldn't. After school the day he got his grade, he took his model out to a field and shot it up with his BB gun.

It wasn't right. Crab didn't give him an A just because of who Curtis was, because of his reputation, because Curtis had an attitude that he didn't like. But that's how it was for Curtis. No one ever gave him a chance. I may have been the last person on the earth that held out any hope for him. And I was about to abandon him. But maybe I could convince him to come back with me. I had to try, anyway.

That night, when I was lying on the floor in my sleeping bag, about to go to sleep, I finally worked up the guts. There wasn't any point to ease into it, so I came out with it: "Maybe we should head back home after we leave here. We're never going to make it to Canada. I mean, who are we kidding?"

Curtis rolled over on the couch toward me. He didn't say anything. He just looked at me. A look that said *I already told you I'm not heading back.* A look that said *I already told you nobody is taking me in.* A look that said *Why would you even ask me that?*

"Okay," I said. I knew it was pointless to discuss it further. I looked down. "Well, I'm heading back home when we leave here."

His eyebrow furrowed. He took a deep breath and nodded. "Okay. I don't blame you." He rolled away and faced the back of the couch. "You should go home."

I turned off the light and twisted onto my side away from him.

# Elvis Dances

I doze, reclining on top of the leaves and blooms of a vast tangle of vines, thick on the ground and soft like a dreamy mattress. Adorned with purple and pink flowers, the coiling vines stretch away from a huge stub of a plant in every direction. I pull the heavy fragrance of the flowers through my nostrils in deep draws.

Elvis stands above me, a black and white image like he stepped out of a television from his appearance on the *Ed Sullivan Show*. An acoustic guitar is held against his gut. He is young. His hair is slick and short. He's wearing black pants and a checkered jacket. He slings the guitar around behind him and grabs me by the collar. His body crackles with static as he pulls me up.

My head rolls back; my eyes drift shut.

He slaps me, back and forth, trying to wake me. "Jack! Jack! What are you doing, Jack? I told you to find me. What the hell are you doing?"

"I'm looking," I say. I weakly swing my head around. My eyes loll in their sockets.

"You looking for me in this patch of weeds? Well, I'm not here."

His face twists for an instant, like the vertical hold lost focus. "You disappoint me, Jack."

"Leave me alone." I close my eyes. "Let me sleep."

"Where's Curtis? Where did you leave him?"

"He's right over there." I look across the patch of vines, expecting to see Curtis nestled comfortably. But he's not there. A deep, empty fear grips my gut like an icy fog piercing into me. Something has happened to him. Something bad. And it's my fault. It's something I could've prevented. I left him alone. I didn't watch him. I didn't stick with him when I should have. "I don't know."

"You better find him, don't you think there, Jack?" Elvis's image twists again, like he's standing in a fun house mirror.

"But I don't know where he is."

"What kind of a friend are you?" Elvis's image realigns.

"I'm not his keeper."

"Not his keeper? He's your best friend. If you don't care enough about him to try to help him then who do you care about?"

"Leave me alone." I snuggle back down into the flowers and vines. They feel soft and inviting.

"I gave you a quest. Don't think I don't know that you're planning to float your ass back home if you ever leave this place. But I don't see that happening anytime soon. You're stuck here. Admit it."

The vines caress me and hold me securely. "I'm not stuck. I'm floating along." I smile, nestling against the soft foliage. "I'm comfortable."

"Floating along. Bullshit! You're stuck, and you can't give up. You have to keep going on."

I turn away from him. I adjust the petals of a flower under my head like I'm fluffing a pillow.

The grip of the plant tightens on me, cutting into my wrists and ankles.

"Hey!"

Tendrils crawl up my legs and coil tightly around my thighs and torso. They're thick like eels. I struggle against them, but I'm bound in place, unable to move. The vines begin dragging me toward the base of the plant that twists itself over and lays its top on the ground. The top begins opening and closing, a huge mouth chomping. I look down the thing's gullet and see row upon row of teeth, quivering and gnashing. The vines drag me toward it. I kick and thrash, trying to keep myself away, to keep myself from being devoured. My hands scrape across the ground, my fingers digging over crumbling, dry earth. "Help me!"

"I thought you wanted me to go away."

I grope at the foliage around me. The leaves and flowers strip through my grasp; vines and stems snap in my hands. My body scuffs across the ground. I'm pulled to the edge of the plant. Its maw gnashes the air inches from my feet. I flail and mange to clutch a sturdy root that juts above the earth. I claw at it furiously and achieve a tenuous hold. The vines continue to pull at me, yanking and yanking at me.

"Elvis! Save me!"

"Save yourself, Jack. I'm going to sing." Elvis jumps back and takes the guitar in his hands. He begins strumming wildly. He starts to sing "Hound Dog." I feel the music pumping in my blood. Energy surges through me. My eyes go wide, fixing on him as he dances around. His legs are jittering, and his arms wave in the air. I climb up off the ground. He floats up and hovers above me. His face is contorted, and his mouth twists to his signature snarl. Light radiates out from him. Watching Elvis perform, I feel all that power that I know exists in him. I want to go to him. I want to find him. I reach out to touch him. The vines snap away from my body. I stagger toward him, breaking free.

Several thick vines stretch like tentacles from the base of the plant and wrap themselves around my hips, my chest, and my neck. They pull me back, skidding across the ground back toward the chomping plant.

"Elvis! Help me! I can't hold on for much longer."

"What are you going to do, Jack? Are you going to look for me?"

"Yes, Elvis. I'll find you. I promise I will."

He rises higher and higher into the air, all the while belting out his song. Behind him, spelled out in bright white bulbs like you would see in Vegas: "GRACELAND."

I gaze back up at Elvis. "Is that where I'll find you? Elvis, is that where I need to go? Graceland?"

"It's a start, Jack. But you have a long road ahead. For now, know this: when things are their darkest, the golden arches shall be your salvation. They shall deliver you from forces that conspire against you. Let that be a sign to you, Jack. Look for the golden arches in your hour of need."

I am only a few feet from the plant. The teeth are loud and buzzing in my ear. "Help me, Elvis!" I am pulled into the opening. I grip its upper jaw with my hands and wedge my legs against its lower jaw. "I can't hold out any longer."

"For Christ's sake, Jack, just wake up. It's only a damn dream."

"Oh."

# *Waiting for Good Dog*

I lay on the floor of Skeeter's trailer, a string of shag carpet, wet with drool, tucked in the corner of my mouth. Skeeter, Minnow, and Curtis sat on the couch, mesmerized by a *Flintstones* episode.

The images from the dream hung clearly in my mind. "Hound Dog" rattled through my head. It all felt so real. Just like the dream I had in the park in Georgia. It made me wonder: Was Elvis really trying to communicate with me? But how could he be? How was that possible? I shook my head. I told myself it meant nothing. It did nothing more than show me how I was feeling. That was all. It was all the emotions raging through my head coming out for a party. That was why it felt so strong. That was why it echoed through me. It didn't change anything. What would the point of going to Graceland be? How could the Golden Arches be my salvation? That was crazy. It made no sense.

I lifted myself off the floor. Curtis stared doll-eyed at the television. Elvis was right about one thing; we needed to get away from here, and the sooner the better. And no matter what Elvis had said to me in the dream or what promises I had made, I wanted to go home. It was time to face up to what we had done. I had taken it as far as I could. But if I couldn't get Curtis to come with me, maybe I could get Curtis away from Skeeter, get him back out on the road. But whether Curtis decided to stay with these drug dealers or not, I was out. I was heading home.

"We need to go! Tomorrow! I mean it."

Curtis wouldn't look at me, but clenched his face in annoyance. I didn't let it go. We argued about it most of the day. I tried to convince him to move on, and I almost did. But that came to an end when Skeeter heard from his guy and the deal was set for that evening. Curtis knew the money would start rolling in again. But I wasn't staying for it. I told Curtis that tomorrow he was taking me to a bus station in Dugan.

Minnow planned to pick Skeeter up at seven to drive him to the deal. But not much went according to plan that night. Around six, Minnow called and said that he couldn't make it. Skeeter was pissed. He griped how it was too late to call it off—his connection, Good Dog, had come in from Georgia.

Curtis was Skeeter's only option. I tried to talk Curtis out of it. But Skeeter dangled a couple hundred bucks in front of him and said how the place was only fifteen minutes away. Curtis agreed to take him. For the money. For his stupid Canada fund. I couldn't let him go alone. I didn't know what I could do if anything happened, but I was going to stay with Curtis, at least until I left him the next day. Funny how that works.

We piled into Curtis's car at 7:30. The meeting was set for eight but Skeeter wanted to get there early, so he had time to scope everything out. He directed us to turn off onto a narrow dirt road, slick from an afternoon rain. Curtis's car bumped over potholes that sprayed muddy water as we drove through them. The road forked, and we veered left. The other fork went up steeply and curved sharply away. We went another half mile. Skeeter told Curtis to get the car turned around. The road was narrow, so Curtis did a three-point turn in about five points. He turned off the car.

"The meeting is right up there." Skeeter pointed up the hill. "Off that other road that split off from this one. That road goes about another mile before it reaches that clearing. You'll be able to see us from here. If there's trouble, we'll have a good head start out of here."

"If there's any trouble, you better get your ass back here in a hurry, because we'll leave you," I said.

Skeeter nodded. "Don't worry, man. This will go smooth as glass. You'll see."

We sat and waited. The hill was picketed with hundreds of tall, thin trees; mud ruts ribbed the slope. The sun set and, as the remaining light melted away, the trees and bushes faded into the hillside. Skeeter got out of the car and paced. The damp leaves whispered under his shuffling feet. He looked up the hill toward the road.

The top of the hill lit up, and a car came to a stop there. Its lights shined out over the edge into the tops of the trees in front of us.

"This is it," Skeeter said. He headed into the woods, disappearing against the dark hillside. Leaves crunched under his feet, and we heard him slip in the mud a couple of times as he climbed. When he reached the top of the hill, his silhouette cut through the shafts of light.

"Hey!" Skeeter said. He put his hands up.

"Man, you scared us," one of them said. I couldn't hear Skeeter's response. The headlights of the car went out, and two car doors opened.

Voices filtered through the woods. They talked low, and I couldn't make out what was being said. I heard what I thought was the sound of a trunk opening, and a light glowed dully at the top of the hill.

"Looks good," Skeeter said. This was followed by more muffled speech. I made out two other people from the tone of the voices. One had a low, harsh voice, and the other talked at a higher pitch and seemed more energetic.

"Someone's coming!" Skeeter yelled.

Cars growled up the road toward them. Lights flooded the area above us, a combination of headlights, spotlights, and flashlights. They waved back and forth through the trees along the hillside. Curtis and I craned our heads out the windows and looked up, trying to get a better view. The shapes of people moved across the shafts of light.

Someone barked, "Nobody move! Keep your hands where I can see them!" All the shapes froze.

"They're getting busted." Curtis gripped the top of the car door. "What are we going to do?"

"I think we should sit tight. They won't see us unless they shine their lights down the hill." I leaned forward in the passenger seat. I shouldn't've come. Why was it so damn important to Curtis? Why didn't he listen to me? About anything.

Voices growled down from the top of the hill. Two of the forms put their hands on top of their heads. The third made a break for it. Leaves rustled like they were being kicked.

"We got a rabbit!" one of the cops yelled.

We heard a splash like someone jumping into a big pile of leaves. "Where do you think you're going?" a cop asked. The leaves crackled like several people were wrestling around in them. Then we heard someone being dragged across the ground. All we could do was sit there and hope they didn't shine their lights down the hill and spot us.

"There should be two cars. Where's the other car?" one cop asked.

"You didn't walk here, did you?" another cop asked.

"N-n-n-no," Skeeter stammered out.

"How did you get here? Huh!"

"A car." Skeeter managed to say.

"What car?"

"Who brought you?"

"J-j-j-jack and C-c-c-curtis."

"Jack and Curtis? Where are they?"

"They're right down there," he said, overcoming his stuttering problem and pointing down toward us.

Spotlights weaved through the trees in front of us. Rays of light sifted through the trees and fell on our car. "There they are," a cop shouted. Two cops tramped down the hill, flashlights bobbing as they came. One slipped on the mud and splashed to the ground on his butt.

"Let's go," I said. My breath caught in my throat. I pushed myself back into my seat, waiting for Curtis to crank the engine and take off. Cops thrashed through the leaves about halfway down the side of the hill.

Curtis seemed frozen. He leaned forward against the steering wheel and his mouth gaped open.

"Come on, Curtis! Let's get out of here!" My eyes swelled as I searched the darkness, expecting cops to appear in front of us at any second, guns waving.

Curtis started the car, popped it into drive, snapped on our headlights, and took off. Our car fishtailed back and forth, then smoothed straight before hitting a deep pothole. My head banged into the roof. In the glow of our taillights, I saw a cop emerge from the brush behind us. I clutched the dash with one hand and wedged the other against the door. The car rattled over the rough dirt road. As we passed where the roads converged, I looked up the right fork. I couldn't see anyone coming.

Our car hit a muddy section of the road and slid down like it was on skis. Curtis's eyes bugged wide, the tendons stuck out on his neck. The back wheels sloshed back and forth. The tires spun wildly, sliding toward the steep edge of the road. I thought we were going to slip off and go tumbling down the bank into the trees. The car regained traction. I glanced back and saw the glow of headlights coming up behind us. When we reached the intersection to the main road, a car drove by.

"Curtis, go the other way. When the cops get here, they'll see a car going in each direction. They won't know which one is us."

Curtis turned right, toward Dugan. We were a couple miles outside of town. The noise of the engine swelled as Curtis's car lumbered up to speed. I looked behind us. A cop car pulled up to the highway. It paused for a minute and headed our way.

"Damn." I faced the front. "They're coming."

Curtis's hands squeezed the wheel tighter.

The moaning of a siren swelled behind us. I looked back to measure the distance between us and the cop car steaming after us with its rollers on. We had at least a mile on them. Our speedometer wobbled around a hundred. The sound of the siren edged louder. We were approaching the town, but it was still a long way off.

"What are we going to do?" Curtis asked, his teeth clenched.

"Do you think they got a good look at our car?" I tried to estimate the rate they were gaining on us. It seemed we would still have some distance on them when we reached town.

Curtis shrugged his shoulders. "It's hard to tell. I'm pretty sure they didn't get our license plate number."

I shook my head. "Skeeter is probably telling them every last detail about us, down to what brand of shorts we have on."

"When we hit Dugan, we'll have to slow down." Curtis pounded the steering wheel. "We're screwed."

"The traffic might be exactly what we need. We could never outrun them. Maybe we can lose them."

We raced toward Dugan and approached the traffic light at the edge of town. It shifted from red to green. As we neared, it turned yellow, then red. Cars started to flow across the intersection, but nobody was in front of us.

"I'm not stopping." Curtis sped toward it; his eyes narrowed; his shoulders pinched forward. The cop was about half a mile behind. I reached out and put my hands on the dash, bracing for any impact when we hit the intersection. Traffic moved steadily past. Trees and buildings on the corner blocked our view of the traffic. All we could do was plow through and hope.

"Turn right on the main drag," I said. "If we make it through the turn, we'll still have some distance on them. They aren't going to see where we're going for maybe a half a minute."

Curtis bulled his way through the red light, slowing only enough to round the corner. I winced, anticipating a collision. He honked his horn as he cut the wheel. A VW bug swerved into the other lane to avoid us. They gave us the finger.

Curtis weaved his way ahead of a few cars. He raced around a Datsun and cut off a pickup truck. I saw them ahead of us: the golden arches, like Elvis had told me about in the dream. They loomed before us on the right. Big and yellow. Could that be our salvation? A McDonald's? There was no way we were going to outrace the cops. But could we hide in the parking lot? It seemed like our only chance. I looked back; the cops hadn't made the turn yet.

"Turn into McDonald's and go through the drive-thru," I said.

"Huh?" Curtis looked at me like I was nuts.

"Just do it. If the cop doesn't see us, it would be the last thing he would expect us to do."

"I don't know. If he spots us, we'll be trapped."

"Do you have a better idea? We can't outrun him."

Curtis paused. "I guess not."

Curtis turned into McDonald's. The tires squealed briefly, then caught. I was flung against the door. The siren grew louder as the cop turned onto the main drag. We drove up to the speaker. Two vans full of softball players pulled in behind us. They blocked any view of us from the road.

"What'll you have?" a voice asked from the speaker.

"Oh." Curtis's voice was shaking. "Ah…two Big Macs, two fries, and two large Cokes."

The siren approached on the main road. It sounded loud, like a train whistle passing through a tunnel. The cop drove by, and the siren faded into the distance.

"That'll be $5.58. Drive to the next window."

Curtis pulled forward, took a ten out of his pocket, and paid for our food. His hand shook as he gave the cashier the bill. We parked the car between two other cars. I threw my head back against the headrest and exhaled.

"Hey, what are you guys doing?" someone asked. I about jumped out of my seat. I turned and saw one of the guys we delivered pot to heading toward us.

"What's up?" Curtis asked the guy. Curtis attempted to jab his straw through the opening in the lid of his Coke. He missed three times before getting it through.

"Nothing, man. Are you guys working tonight? I'm getting a little low."

A cop car drove by. He paused, searching the parking lot, but we were blocked from his view by the other cars.

"No, there's nothing going on." I watched the cop car through the window of the car next to us. If he recognized us, it would be all over. There was no way we could escape from the parking lot.

"Bummer. Well, keep me in mind next time you're out." The guy walked away. The cop drove on.

"What are we going to do now?" Curtis asked.

"Finish our burgers and drive out of town like nothing's going on." I reached into the bag and pulled out my food. I handed Curtis the bag with his food in it.

We sat there and ate. Two more cop cars drove by with people nested in the back seats. I thought I recognized Skeeter in the second one.

"I thought I saw Minnow sitting in the front of one of those cars." Curtis shoveled a handful of fries into his mouth.

"Are you sure?" I paused before cramming the burger into my mouth.

He nodded. "Pretty damn sure. Skinny, pale guy with stringy black hair. Who else could it be?"

I remembered when we were delivering pot and that guy asked Minnow about the cops pulling him over. Minnow blew it off and said they were just hassling him. But I bet he got busted that night he ditched Skeeter. That's why Skeeter was stranded on the road. And I bet Minnow worked some deal with the cops to get off easier by agreeing to set up Skeeter and his connection. They probably would've arrested us at Skeeter's if the crown jewel of the bust weren't Good Dog.

Minnow betrayed Skeeter, betrayed his best friend. Sold him

out. They talked about what great friends they were. What a bunch of crap. I looked at Curtis. Wasn't I doing the same thing to him? Leaving him to his fate. Abandoning him. I felt guilty as hell.

I needed to try to help him. I needed to stick with him and see things through. If I abandoned him now, I'd regret it, especially if anything bad happened to him. I'd know that I had given up on him. I'd know that maybe I could've done more to save him. He still had a chance to find something that would help him turn himself around, something that would allow him to face up to what we had done. Elvis was right about that.

Elvis was right about the Golden Arches too. They were our salvation. I never would've thought about pulling in and hiding from the cops if I hadn't had that dream. And if there were some truth to the dream, then maybe there was some truth to the rest of it. Maybe Elvis was out there somewhere, leading me to him somehow, leading me toward something. And whatever that something was, it spoke to what twisted at my heart, to what wound me up inside. And maybe that was at Graceland. And maybe Curtis would find what he needed to get himself straight if we could make it there, make it to Graceland. I had to hope for that, anyway. And even though I wasn't entirely convinced, I wanted to know for sure. I needed to know for sure. And there was only one way to do that.

For the first time since we had set out, I knew where I was headed. I knew it with a certainty I hadn't had with anything else in my life.

I ate the last bite of my Big Mac and stuffed the empty container into the bag. Curtis started the Dart, and we drove out of town.

"So I guess we can find a town with a bus station tomorrow and put you on a bus back home?" Curtis asked.

"No."

"No?"

"We're going to Graceland," I said.

Curtis cocked his eyebrow at me and turned to face the road. He looked ahead, digesting what I said, then smiled.

# *Insomnia*

"Graceland? You sure? I thought you wanted to head back home."

"I changed my mind."

Curtis took a deep breath and shook his head. "You should go home. The longer you stay with me, the deeper in you'll get. You were right to want to leave me."

"No."

"Why?"

"I want to go to Graceland."

"Why?"

"I don't know. I just do." It wasn't anything that I could talk about with Curtis. Not without him laughing his ass off at me. I couldn't tell him about the dreams. He wouldn't believe me. He would think I was nuts, and part of me would've agreed with him.

"Okay." Curtis paused and looked out the window. "You know, my dad went there. He met Elvis."

I had heard Curtis tell me this story a hundred times, probably as many times as Curtis's father had told him the story, but I let him go on.

"Dad was standing in front of the gate with a bunch of people wanting to see him. People did that every day, hoping to catch a glimpse of the King. Dad was chatting with one of the guards when Elvis rode up to the gate on a horse. Dad said he stood there looking straight up at Elvis. 'Nice day. Isn't it?' Elvis asked my dad. Dad said they talked for a few minutes, about nothing, really. 'Well, I'll be seeing you.' Elvis leaned down and shook his hand. Then he rode off. After he left, Dad wrote on the fence, '4\17\71—the day I met Elvis.' He put his initials below it."

"That's pretty cool."

He smiled at me. "You think what he wrote will still be there? That would be neat as shit, seeing what Dad wrote about Elvis."

I shook my head. "It's been a long time, Curtis. That has probably worn away by now."

"Yeah, but I can look anyway."

"Yeah, looking is free."

We drove through the night. All we wanted to do was get away from Dugan, as far as possible. From the time we spent with Skeeter, we were both wasted, burnt out, whatever you want to call it. The varying double-yellow and dashed-white lines passed through our vision like a hypnotist's spiraling wheel.

The first hour, I pulled out the atlas and mapped our path up Alabama toward Tennessee. But as the night wore on, we took one turn and then another. We lost our way. It was too dark to see the atlas, and we were too tired to stop and try to figure it out. We just wanted to keep going. We drove without any direction. All we wanted to do was get further along. One more mile, we kept telling ourselves. One more mile down the road. One more mile away from the lives we left behind. One more mile closer to Graceland. We followed our headlights and chased the road in front of us. Always gaining that one more mile, but never getting any closer to where we wanted to go.

In the dark dead of morning, still mired in Alabama somewhere, we stopped at a Stop N' Shop. We needed gas, and I wanted a cup of coffee.

We pulled in beside a gas pump. Fluorescent lights radiated a bleached glow over the cement parking lot splotched with different shades of motor oil. A moth thumped into the metal roof of a canopy over the pumps like it was trying to pound its way through.

A red Chevy Impala with a black hood was parked in front of the store with North Carolina plates. Along the top of the windshield and the back window, small knit balls dangled. A guy leaned forward in the driver's seat; his face was buried in his arms, his hands clutched the top of the steering wheel.

Curtis and I rolled out of the Dart. I staggered a couple of steps, stretching stiffness out of my body.

Curtis twisted the cap off the gas tank. I walked toward the store. The guy in the car sat up straight and started muttering. Inside the store, a girl walked in front of the coolers that lined the back wall. She was a tall, thin girl wearing a tank top and tight bell-bottoms. She had long, thin auburn hair.

I went in and told the cashier to turn on the pump. Then I followed the smell of burnt coffee to a glass carafe with coffee the consistency of ink. No way I was drinking that. "Can I make a fresh pot?" I asked. The cashier nodded.

I rinsed out the pot and searched through the cabinets. I found the packs of coffee and filters. I took a filter and dropped it into the basket and picked up one of the cellophane coffee packs. I tried to tear it open, but it wouldn't tear. I tried yanking it open at the seam, but it wouldn't budge. I could've pulled harder, but I was afraid the pack would explode and shower coffee everywhere.

I was considering what to do next when the girl with the long hair came up to me.

"Let me help you," she said. A beam of skin showed between her hip-hugging jeans and the blue tank top she wore. She set down a bag of chips and a soda. She took the coffee pack from my hand, pinched the shiny cellophane, and tore it open with ease. "You were trying too hard."

"Thanks," I said.

"You shouldn't try so hard. Sometimes, you have to know how to apply just the right amount of pressure to get what you want." I couldn't help but smile. She wasn't beautiful or anything, but there was something about her. To me, anyway.

"Thanks," I said.

She handed me the open coffee pack and placed her hand on my arm. "You know what they say, one good turn deserves another." She flipped her head, glancing to the parking lot and throwing her hair over her shoulder.

"What do you mean?"

"Can you help me with a little problem?"

My body tensed. We had just run from the cops. I didn't want to get involved with anything, especially anything that was a problem. "What?"

"You see that guy?" She nodded over her shoulder to the guy in the parking lot. "The one sitting behind the wheel of the Impala."

"Yeah."

"I need to get away from him."

I shrugged. "If you want to get away from him, then leave him."

"I don't think it will be that easy. He's been drinking. And he's being a little…possessive. I think he gets angry when he drinks."

I rolled my eyes. "Look, I really don't want to get between you and your boyfriend, and—"

"He's not my boyfriend." She crossed her arms. "I'm just catching a ride with him."

"Then what's the big deal then?"

"Well, we've been riding together two days now. He's developed an attachment. He thinks there's more between us than there is. And like I said, he's been drinking."

That guy looked like trouble. "What are you expecting me to do anyway? If you want to leave him, tell him you're leaving him and leave. I don't have to go with you, holding your hand."

"I'm a good judge of character and—"

"Then what are you doing with that guy?"

She paused, cocked her head, and looked me over. Her eyes stopped on mine, and I met them. I felt her peering into me, probing beyond my eyes to the inside, getting a glimpse at the me within me. She turned away. My gaze reached after hers.

She leaned back and grinned a smug little grin like she had seen something in me, something that maybe I didn't know existed. She had looked into me and found the person she hoped to find, and maybe it was the person I wanted to be. I don't know. But whatever she saw, she knew I would help her, if it came to it, if she needed my help. She was right. That smug grin of hers pissed me off. Somehow I felt like I was being used.

She nodded. "I'll try just telling him. Let's see how it goes." She walked away, leaving the chips and soda on the counter.

I poured the coffee into the basket and started it brewing. She went to the Impala and leaned in toward his open window. I saw her talking, but I couldn't hear what was said through the store window. Her hand was waving in the air. The guy nodded, but had a confused and pained look on his face.

He wore a baseball cap and had a thick brown mustache that hung over his upper lip. The girl stopped talking and took a step back from the car. She kept her attention on the guy as he took in what she had told him. He scowled, shook his head, and got out of the car, bumping his baseball cap on the car door. The cap fell to the pavement. He bent to pick it up. His blue jean jacket spread open, and I noticed a large, oval, silver belt buckle with "Eddie" across it. He started talking loudly to her, not quite yelling, but almost. He moved toward her, and she backed away.

I looked to see where Curtis was. He had finished pumping the gas and sat in the driver's seat of the Dart with his head leaned back against the headrest.

The guy stretched his arm toward the girl and grabbed her by the wrist. She tried to twist away from him, but he held on firmly. He started shouting at her.

"Shit," I said.

I left the coffee brewing and went to them.

"I don't want any trouble," the cashier said as I passed the counter.

"Tell that to them." I walked out the door.

Eddie was bent over, clutching her arm. The girl leaned away from him, trying to pry herself away. It looked like an odd game of Tug of War.

"Let me go!"

"Becky! You can't leave me! You can't!"

"Get over it, Eddie."

"Buddy, why don't you let her go?" I asked.

He turned to me, lifting Becky's hand to the height of his shoulder. "Mind your own business." Eddie's head wobbled. I could smell the beer on him.

"She doesn't want to stay with you. You've had too much to drink. You should crawl into the back of your car and sleep it off."

"Don't tell me what to do! I love this girl."

"Well, you need to let her go."

"No! I won't." Pain racked his face. His body swayed in an opposite direction than his head wobbled, keeping him oddly balanced. He looked back to the girl. "Becky. Please."

"Let me go, Eddie. I told you, I'm leaving." She cocked her hip to the side and leaned away from him.

"Give me another chance." He turned toward her.

"Another chance? You didn't have a first chance. I hardly even know you." She tried to pull away from him.

"I know I can make you happy." Eddie held his ground, holding firm to her arm. "Becky, how can you do this to me?"

"You're drunk." She yanked her hand out of his grasp and danced away from him. I stepped in between them.

Curtis got out of our car and made his way toward us. Curtis outweighed the guy by about fifty pounds. I hoped Curtis would keep his cool.

"We can work through this." Eddie tried to step around me to get to Becky, but I moved into his way. "I'll be lost without you."

She shook her head. "Get over it." A few strands of her long, shiny, auburn hair fell across her left eye. She rolled her head to the side and swept it back.

"You need to let her go, Eddie," I said.

"No." Eddie reached toward her.

I put my hands on his shoulders to hold him back. "She doesn't want to go with you," I said.

He pushed into me, shoving me back a step. "You going to make me?" He poked me in the chest with his finger.

I moved back and put my hands up in front of myself. The last thing I wanted was to fight him. "Look. I don't want any trouble."

Curtis edged closer. He kept his eyes focused on Eddie and crouched slightly like a bull ready to charge.

Becky walked around to the other side of the car. Her high platform clogs clopped on the cement. She reached in through the open window and grabbed her backpack. It had a sleeping bag tied to the base.

Eddie took a step toward me. He put his fists up. "This is all your fault. She wouldn't have left me if you didn't butt in." He took a swing at me. I saw it coming and easily stepped out of the way.

But that was all Curtis needed to see. He lowered his shoulder and charged. "Hey Eddie," he said.

Eddie turned. Curtis plowed into him, going full speed. It was like watching a freight train plow through a house of cards.

Eddie sprawled back across the asphalt, skidding to a stop on the seat of his jeans. He rolled over onto his knees. His chest heaved. Curtis leaned over him, his body tensed and his hands clenched into fists. Eddie gasped, trying to draw breath back into his body.

"Curtis, settle down."

Curtis's eyes were wild. I could see the adrenaline pumping through him. He looked at me. "What the hell are you doing getting involved in this mess?"

Becky marched across the parking lot toward the road.

The cashier poked his head out the door. "I'm calling the cops. I told you that I didn't want any trouble." He went back to the counter and picked up the phone.

"Shit!" I said.

"Let's get the hell out of here," Curtis said.

Eddie lay on the ground, holding himself up with one arm and cradling his mid-section with the other. He looked to the highway, toward Becky walking away. He tried to call her name. He didn't have his wind back, so it came out in a broken gasp.

She paused, glanced back at Eddie, then turned away like she was doing nothing more than noticing some gum stuck to the bottom of her shoe. When she reached the highway, she held out her hand with her thumb pointed up to a passing car.

Eddie stumbled to his feet, his arm still across his gut. He staggered after her. His eyes were open wide; then his brows crinkled like he was going to cry.

"We need to get out of here." Curtis turned and took a step toward our car. "Come on. The cops are coming."

I didn't move. I kept my gaze on Eddie.

He raised his hand toward Becky. "Don't leave me! I don't want to be alone anymore. You don't know what it's like. I get so lonely sometimes."

Becky kept making her way down the highway.

Eddie gave up. "She's gone." He turned toward me. "Gone." He crumbled to his knees and hung his head. Eddie shuddered as he started to cry. "I don't believe it." He shook his head back and forth.

Curtis grabbed my shoulder. "Come on."

I shook Curtis's hand off. "Let's help him to his car."

"We need to get out of here!" Curtis said. "That cashier called the cops."

I knew we needed to get out of there, but I didn't want to leave Eddie. Not like that. Not the way he was. I felt bad for him. Even though he was drunk and even though he deserved to have Becky take off and Curtis run over him like a steamroller. A part of me understood how he felt. I stepped up to Eddie. I put my hand on his back.

He lifted his head and thumped his palm on my chest. Tears welled in his eyes. "Will you help me?"

"Yeah, I'll help you. Come on, buddy." I pulled him to his feet. He slung his arm over my shoulder.

"You're not a bad fella." He looked at me.

"Okay. You need to sleep it off." I walked him to his car.

He grimaced. "Oh God! My woman left me at the...uh . . ." He paused to read the store's sign. ". . . Stop N' Shop, and you want me to sleep it off? I need to howl." He howled at the top of his lungs. He sounded like a bloodhound with an upset stomach.

Curtis threw his head back. "Good lord."

"Curtis, help me get him into his car."

"We need to get out of here."

"Then help me. It won't take long."

Curtis came over and took his other arm. We eased Eddie into his Chevy.

"I'm all alone." He lay on the back seat, sputtering and sobbing. He issued another howl; this one choked in his throat. "Nothing worse than being alone on the road. I had her in my life. Everything felt so different. Everything felt right. You know." He looked at me and nodded. His wide silver belt buckle glinted in the light from the store. "For a while." He shook his head. "She abandoned me. Tomorrow, she won't even remember who I was. I'll be back on the road. It's always so far, when you got no place to go and you got no one." Eddie lay sprawled across the back seat.

He stared up. "Look at me." Mirrors covered the roof in uneven squares that were angled with the contour of the ceiling. They reflected multiple broken images of his face. "What's left for me? There's nothing there." He looked at himself and shook his head. "Nothing there." He stared blankly upward with an empty gaze. "I wish I was dead."

"It's all right. You'll feel better tomorrow."

He closed his eyes.

I understood Eddie, feeling alone and everything, feeling like there was a big gap in your…I don't know…in your soul, I guess. I'd spent most of my life feeling that way, alone, without anyone or anything that I really cared about or any place where I felt I belonged, but I wanted something. Loneliness can creep up on you. It can twist you up inside. Make you do stupid crap like put mirrors on the ceiling of your car. Make you think you have some kind of a connection with someone you hardly know. In the end, it can make you feel like you have nothing. That was sure how Eddie felt.

I followed Curtis back to our car. I looked up the highway. The brake lights of a passing truck came on, and it squealed to a stop, just past Becky. The door popped open. She jogged to the truck, pulled herself up into the cab, and closed the door. The brakes gave a final exhalation, and it drove away.

Curtis started the Dart. We pulled out, falling in behind the truck.

"What the hell happened?" Curtis asked.

I told him about what the girl said to me in the store.

"Typical," Curtis said. "She was using you to get away from that guy. That bitch. She almost got us busted. She got us into that mess, then took off."

*That wasn't all she did,* I thought. My eyes locked on the taillights of the truck in front of us. We followed it for two miles before it turned off. I watched the taillights until they disappeared from view. I wondered where she was headed. I didn't think that I would ever see her again, and that made me sad. I didn't know then that our paths would cross again, and that without Becky's help Curtis and I never would've made it to Graceland.

# *Stumped*

Curtis stopped at the junction for Highway 331. It was just after five in the morning, and there wasn't another soul on the road. He put the car in park. "Okay, so where the hell are we?"

I grabbed the atlas and opened it. Curtis turned on the inside car light, which was almost as bright as a dead firefly. I barely made out the page that was Alabama. I thought I found 331. And I thought I figured out where we were. "We can take this all the way to Montgomery," I said. "Turn right."

Curtis headed up the road. Morning light was leaking into the sky, and Curtis drove fast, trying to make up for all the time we'd lost. Cool air rushed through the open window, full of moisture from the morning dew. That seemed to wake me up a little. I never got my coffee at that store. Probably just as well.

We had gone about twenty miles when something came in through the window and smacked against the back seat.

"What was that?" Curtis asked.

"I don't know." I turned around to look.

A brown lump lay on the back seat. It started moving. I turned, knelt on my seat and looked closer. The thing righted itself and crawled toward me with its wings.

"It's a bat."

After that, everything happened in a blur. The car went around a turn. I grabbed the headrest to keep my balance. The bat tumbled across the seat, bouncing off the door and into the air. It clawed and flailed and twisted into flight.

Curtis hunched his shoulders and leaned forward. He pressed himself against the steering wheel. The bat lurched toward me. I fell back against the dashboard and screamed. It veered from me and flew into the windshield in front of Curtis. It slid into the crevice between the dashboard and the windshield and got stuck. It began flapping madly. I turned and flopped back into my seat.

The bat took off and slapped into the center of Curtis's face. Curtis screamed and batted it away with the back of his hand. It sailed across the car and hit the rear window. It squeaked like a rubber mouse and landed on the back seat.

Our car dipped off the road. Curtis slammed on the brakes. The car smashed through a fence, snapping several of the fence posts. It slid across the yard toward a wide stump.

The front end of the car went up. The underside screeched as it scraped against wood. The car rattled as it ground to a stop; the front end settled down like a scale finding balance. Curtis and I rocked forward with the sudden stop. I banged my head on the roof. We snapped back in our seats. The bat flew out the window.

"Crap!" I reached up and felt my forehead. A knot was forming above my hairline. "You about cracked my skull with your driving. Why didn't you stop?"

"I don't know. It all happened so fast. We took out a fence. We probably messed up our car."

"What are you guys doing?" A small boy, probably about seven, looked up at us. "Get your car out of my front yard." Something was wrong. The kid seemed lower than he should be. The car was above the ground somehow, like something had lifted us up.

A screen door screeched open from the front of the house. A woman stood in the doorway, holding a baby in one arm. She stared at us with the tips of her fingers over her open mouth. I opened my car door, and the ground was about a half a foot lower than it should've been. I hopped down. Curtis did the same.

Our car rested on the stump, all four wheels off the ground. It looked like a figure on top of a trophy. I stood there looking at it, wondering how in the world we were going to get our car down, wondering if we could get anywhere without running into trouble.

"Are you boys all right?" The woman stepped forward. The screen door clapped shut behind her. She shifted her baby's weight against her hip. She was pretty, I guessed in her twenties, with thick brown hair. The baby wore nothing but a diaper.

"We're fine." I walked around to the front of the car and stood next to Curtis. He folded his arms across his chest and shook his head.

"Look what you did to our fence." She spoke slowly, with a southern accent. The baby she held squirmed against her, arching its back and straightening its arms, trying to push away from her.

"We lost control of our car," I said.

The little boy stood at the end of a trail his bare feet made through the morning dew. He was a skinny kid wearing a pair of denim shorts and a T-shirt with a faded smiley face on it. Light brown freckles flecked his cheeks. He cupped several small green army men in his hands and gazed down at them.

"A bat flew in the window." Curtis put his hands on his hips. "It flew right in my face."

She held the baby with one hand and freed the tape with the other. She pressed the tape back in place against the diaper. "Look at our yard too. What a mess!"

Our wheels had gouged ruts through the yard up to the stump. Three posts lay broken on the ground. The wire that was strung between them was twisted underneath the car and stretched back to the section of fence still standing. The front end of our car was smashed in.

She reached up and pulled back loose strands of hair that had fallen across her eyes. "You all need to fix it. And you better fix it before my husband gets home. He's going to be very upset."

"Your husband?"

"He gets off his shift at nine. He won't like this. Not at all." The baby started to cry and nuzzled against her neck.

An alarm bell went off in my head. I could think of only a few jobs that required night shifts: hospital workers, firemen, factory workers, and, of course, cops. Maybe there was a factory nearby. "His shift?"

She ignored my question. "There's fence posts and wire in the barn. There might even be a jack or something you can use to get your car down. I need to tend to my baby." She turned to go back inside. "You need to take care of it." She pulled open the door and stepped in.

"So does your husband work at a factory?"

She continued into the house. The screen door clapped shut behind her.

I looked at Curtis.

The little boy sat down in the grass and played with his army men.

"So what does your daddy do?" I asked.

The boy looked at me and smiled with pride. "He's a trooper."

Curtis snapped his head toward the kid. "Your dad's a what?"

"A state trooper." He paused and said the next part carefully, like he had been taught to say it. "An officer of the law. And you better fix our fence like my momma said or you'll be in trouble."

Curtis looked at me.

My shoulders sagged, and the breath went out of me. It seemed hopeless. Our car was stuck. We weren't going anywhere. And how could we get it down? That lady said there was a car jack in the barn, but we would need a lot more than that to get our car off the stump. And we only had a couple hours to figure something out before the law came down on us. But all we could do was try. I didn't want to give up. I wanted to make it to Graceland, and if that meant getting our stupid car off that stump, I sure as hell was going to give it my best. I shrugged. "You heard the kid. We better get on it." I headed toward the barn.

Curtis was right behind me. "I don't believe this. How can this stuff keep happening to us?"

"I don't know, Curtis."

"What are we going to do? Did you look at it? Holy shit! We'd need a forklift to get it off that stump. We're screwed."

"Let's see what's in the barn. Maybe we can figure something out." Even though I said that, I pretty much agreed with Curtis: We were screwed.

The red paint on the barn was chipped and peeling in places. I lifted up a board that lay across brackets on each door and dropped it to the side. Curtis pulled open one of the doors that groaned as he dragged it across the grass. It was dark inside, the only light entering from the doorway. The barn was ripe with the smell of wet fertilizer and old hay. Several fence posts and a roll of wire lay along the wall.

"Look." I pointed at a stack of concrete blocks. They sat back in the shadows underneath the loft among a collection of tools, barrels, and house furniture, all of it dumped in a pile. "Those blocks might be something we can use." I walked toward them.

"Yeah, maybe, but we're going to need more than that." Curtis moved a rusted spring mattress out of the way to get at the blocks. We carried them to the doorway, two at a time. "He's probably the cop that got the call to the Stop N' Shop. That would be just our luck."

"Well then, we better hurry the hell up and get out of here." I went underneath the loft of the barn to look for more stuff we could use. I came across a mechanic's jack buried under a pile of junk. "Jackpot!" I grabbed the handle of the jack and pulled it free. Several items clattered to the floor. There was so much stuff in that barn I was beginning to think that anything we needed would be in there if we looked long enough.

Curtis found a couple of car ramps beside an old washing machine. "I don't like this at all."

"What's to like about it?"

He moved a bunch of gardening tools that lay scattered over the ramps. "If we can get our car down, I say we do that and get the hell out of here. Screw fixing the fence. If that trooper gets home, we're done."

I rolled the jack to the doorway and dropped the handle. It thumped onto the wooden floor of the barn. "We don't know that, Curtis. If we don't fix that damn fence, they'll be after us for sure."

"They're after us anyway. What does one more thing matter? This sucks." Curtis grumbled and shook his head. He picked up one of the car ramps. He held it above his head as he stepped carefully around the junk and set it in the doorway, then went back for the other.

Once we had everything collected by the door, it took several trips to carry the things out to our car. With the items we had—the ramps, the jack, a small shovel, and about twenty cement blocks—we came up with a plan to free our ride. The little boy had gone back into the house. It was a little before eight. We needed to hurry because we had a lot to do.

We started by digging out behind the back wheels just enough so we could slide a block under each. We lay more behind, setting them in a line for the tires to ride across so we could back off the stump. After the blocks, we set the car ramps.

We used more blocks and started to make a platform at the front of the car. Something we could set the jack on and provide enough height for us to jack the front end of the car off the stump.

The little boy came out the screen door and stood in front of us. "Mama said it was all right for me to watch." He looked at me, waiting for approval. He had a bunch of army men pressed against his stomach.

I nodded.

He dropped the army men, sat down in the grass, and began playing with them.

As Curtis and I hauled blocks to the front of the car to make our platform, the boy asked us question after question: "Where are you going?" "What kind of car is that?" "How big was the bat that flew in the window?" "Have you ever been arrested before?" Curtis and I stayed focused on our task. Curtis put the last block in place for the platform. I set the jack on top of it.

"So does your daddy always come straight home from work, or does he go out to breakfast or anything?" I asked.

"My daddy always comes right home. Sometimes real fast. With his lights on and everything. Momma makes him breakfast. Pancakes. I like pancakes. Did you know my daddy shot a man once?"

"Was he a robber or murderer or something?" I asked.

"No." The kid shook his head. "My daddy said it was someone who didn't do what they were told. He shot him good too. Dead."

Curtis looked at me.

I started pumping the jack handle. The jack pushed up into the underside of the car. The front of the car stretched up, and the back wheels pressed down into the blocks we had wedged under them. The front end lifted clear of the stump and sat at an angle on the blocks in back and the car jack.

"My daddy says, a policeman tells you to do something you better do it." He held one of his army men up. "Pow! Pow! My daddy says that some people don't deserve to live."

The car was now completely suspended above the stump. Our plan was working well so far. It felt kind of exciting, actually. I didn't think we would get this far. But we were running out of time; it was already eight-thirty. We had to hurry.

We stacked two blocks under each of the front wheels and set more blocks in stacks behind those; then we lowered the car so the wheels rested on the blocks.

Curtis climbed up into our car carefully. We were afraid that the blocks holding up the front of the car would tilt out and topple, and we would be back where we started. Curtis cranked the engine. He backed the car up as slowly as he could. I watched to make sure the bottom wasn't going to hit the stump. The stacks of blocks held as the wheels groaned over them. When the front of the car cleared the stump, Curtis stopped; I reduced the height of blocks for the front wheels to one and lined them up with the blocks we used for the back wheels. The front wheels thumped down to the shorter stack, and the back wheels rolled off the cinder blocks onto the car ramps and to the ground; the front wheels followed. Curtis drove the car out of the front yard. We had done it.

Curtis waved me over. I walked to his open window and leaned down. It was a little after nine. The trooper would be on his way home.

"Come on," he said. "Let's take off."

"No. We need to fix the damn fence."

"Screw that. Let's get out of here. If Johnny Law gets home, it'll be all over for us."

"No, they'll be after us."

"So what. They're already after us. He's going to bust us for sure when he gets here. You heard that kid. This guy's a real hardass."

If we took off, that cop would get on his radio and have some of his trooper buddies pull us over. We would be stopped before we got fifty miles. But honestly, there was a part of me that didn't want to leave until we fixed the fence. Curtis could pound sand. We broke it. We didn't know the guy would bust us. He might not be that mad if we were trying to make things right, but he sure as hell would be mad if we took off. He sure as hell would want to see us busted then. "We need to fix the fence!"

Curtis pounded his fist in frustration on the steering wheel. "Get in the car!"

"No! You can help me or not, but I'm not leaving without fixing that damn fence."

Curtis cursed under his breath, slammed the car into park, and climbed out.

"Come on, it won't take long." Curtis and I lugged the stuff back to the barn. I grabbed three fence posts, and Curtis grabbed the roll of wire. We started to pull the broken fence posts out of the ground. We had to dig out a little on the sides of each post to loosen them, but they came out easily.

"Daddy!" the boy screamed. We saw the state trooper's car headed up the road.

Curtis scowled at me. He took one of the fence posts and jammed it into the hole. He shoved it in as deep as it would go and packed loose dirt around it.

The trooper's car crunched to a stop in front of us. He got out and surveyed the ruts gouged through the yard and the broken fence. "What the hell happened here?" He walked across the yard, leaning forward, his chest pushed out and his arms behind him. The lady was right. He wasn't happy.

"Sorry, sir," I said. "We lost control of our car. A bat flew in the window. We ran off the road."

His eyes bit into me. "A bat." It was more a statement that he thought I was lying than a question.

"Yes, sir."

Curtis continued working. He jammed another fence post into an open hole.

The lady stepped out of the house. "You're home."

The man ignored her and walked up to me. His eyes locked on mine, piercing me like he was trying to burn holes through my skull. "You boys been drinking?"

"No sir." I straightened and looked ahead. I felt like a private being drilled by a sergeant on the first day of boot camp.

Curtis kept working on the fence, on the last broken fence post. He used the shovel to dig around the edges of the broken post. I was glad the trooper stayed focused on me. I knew Curtis's temper would bust out if he caught a blast of the trooper's hot stare. And it *was* a hot stare. I could feel sweat beginning to collect on my forehead.

"What really happened?"

I turned toward him. "I told you, a bat flew in the window."

"Uh, huh." He took a step to the side of me, inching his face in closer to mine. "I heard there was a call at the Stop N' Shop on Old Coon Road thirty miles from here. There was a fight there. Same kind of car you guys are driving. You know anything about that?"

I felt my jaw set tight and every muscle in my body tensed. I needed to be careful with my answer. If I lied and he knew I was lying, he might take us down just because I lied, but if I told him the truth he might take me down anyway. Our whole trip hung in the balance. I could sense it. If I gave him the wrong answer, an answer he didn't like, it would be over. It would be the end of the line.

"That was us," I said. Curtis rolled his eyes. "This drunk guy tried to pick a fight with us. We put him to bed in the back of his car. That's all that happened. We went on our way."

I felt the eyes of the cop boring into me, searching me, like he was trying to determine the truth for himself. "That's what I heard too. When they got there, the guy was sleeping it off. Probably a good thing, as drunk as he was."

The woman went up to her husband. "They seem like nice boys." She put her hand on his arm. "Why don't you take your shower, and I'll make you some breakfast?"

He grunted and turned away from me to his wife. He seemed to soften a bit. He looked tired. "Okay."

He turned back toward me. "You better be done by the time I've finished my breakfast." He nodded and went into the house. The door slammed shut after him.

It didn't take very long to replace the last fence post and string up new wire. When we were done, we walked up to the house and rapped on the door. I could hear the shower going in the house. I was glad. I didn't want to talk to that trooper again. The lady came out. She had changed into a blue, polka-dot, cotton dress and had her hair in a ponytail.

She looked at the fence. "That looks wonderful." She put her hand on Curtis's forearm. "Thank you." She smiled pleasantly at him. Curtis smiled back.

She looked over her shoulder. The shower turned off. "You guys best get going."

We headed to the car. A puddle of oil was swelling from beneath it.

"Curtis, we broke something. The car's dripping oil."

He got down, rolled to his back and wiggled under the car. "Dang." He got off the ground. Oil ran down his hand. He wiped it on the wet grass. "What are we going to do?"

"We need to get it fixed."

Curtis leaned against the car and bowed his head. "That's going to eat our cash. It keeps getting worse."

"Is there a garage around here where we can take our car?" I asked.

"There's a mechanic just up highway 331. Where you all headed?" She leaned her hip against the railing on the porch steps and placed both hands on the bar.

"North."

"North?" she asked.

"Yeah, we're on our way to Tennessee."

"You all are going the wrong way." She pointed in the direction our car was headed. "The Florida state line is only about ten more miles that way."

I could feel Curtis glaring at me. He was no longer smiling. I refused to look at him.

"Which way is Montgomery?" I asked.

"Back the way you were coming, about ninety miles."

"Ninety miles?" Curtis said.

I shrugged. I didn't care if he was mad. I didn't care if he was blaming me. It takes two to drive around lost all night.

We got in the car and drove off. The night had been a disaster. It had started with the cops chasing us and us almost getting busted and gone on to us getting into a fight and almost getting busted and then finished with us smashing up our car and almost getting busted. In between that, we had wandered around lost and had actually gotten farther away from our destination.

And now we needed to deal with the car trouble; there was no way we would make it to Memphis leaking oil like we were.

But somehow, even with as shitty as everything had gone, I felt good. When I first looked at our car sitting up there, I didn't think we had any hope of getting it down. I thought that we were done. But Curtis and I, we worked together. We had to. And we did. We figured it out. We got his damn car down. I mean, that was something.

And even the thing with fixing the fence—we took care of it, even though we were the ones who smashed it up to begin with and even though it was fix it or get arrested. We fixed it. And we could drive by in two years and still see the fence posts we had put in the ground standing there, unless someone else had rammed them over by then.

So even though our car was all smashed up now and leaking oil and there was a slight grinding coming from the engine, we were still on the road, we were still on our way, still headed to Graceland.

# *Broken Down*

Two miles down the road, a wooden sign dangled from a post, "Carl's Repair Shop" painted on it in black. We turned into a narrow driveway that led past a two-story house. Opposite the house, a man pulled boards from a pile of debris that appeared to be the remains of a garage that had been torn down. He threw them into the bed of a big truck. A new garage stood beside the house. It was freshly painted; the windowpanes of the bay doors were shiny and dust-free and still had yellow stickers angled in the corners. Centered above the doors, an Alabama license plate hung.

Curtis parked, and we got out and walked toward the man.

The day had grown hot. I squinted from the sunlight reflecting off the sand in the driveway. "Are you Carl?"

"Yup. What can I help you with?" He was a tall, thin man in his late forties with a flattop haircut. His eyes were bright blue. They almost seemed like they were glowing, they were so damn bright. His skin was creased and tan like he'd spent a lot of his life working in the sun.

"We're leaking oil. We need to get it fixed," Curtis said.

Carl knelt on the ground and looked under the car. "Looks like you cracked the oil pan." He got up, brushing the sand off his knees, then his hands.

I paused, waiting for him to say something more, but he never did. "Can you fix it?"

"Sure. I have to put in a new oil pan." He took out a handkerchief and wiped the sweat from his forehead.

"How much?" Curtis asked.

Carl pinched his chin with his index finger and thumb. "Around two hundred."

That was about all our cash.

"Let's get out of here." Curtis stepped toward our car.

Carl turned and went back to his work.

I stepped in front of Curtis and put my hand on his chest to stop him. "We can't go on with the car the way it is."

Curtis scuffed his foot in the dirt. A thin tan cloud rose from the ground. "He's trying to take us for all our money. He knows we're stuck." The sound of boards being pulled apart groaned through the air. Curtis tried to step away from me.

I grabbed his shoulder, holding him there. "I've got an idea." I walked over to Carl. "I'll make a deal with you. We'll give you a hundred, and we'll break down the rest of that old garage while you're fixing our car."

He looked over at the big pile of lumber and then at our car. "I can go for that. That's one heck of a deal."

Carl put our car up on the lift. Curtis and I started to work. Carl gave us each a pair of cotton gloves to wear. We pried planks and two-by-fours off the larger support beams and threw them on the truck. The first few tolled on the metal floor of the truck bed. As the bed filled, the boards slapped together as they dropped in. A dust stirred around us as we worked, a thick dust that had settled into the wood from all the years the structure stood. It got in our noses and eyes and seemed to fill the pores of our sweating skin.

Carl's tools clanked and scraped against metal while he worked. Loud country music echoed through the garage. I think it was Hank Williams. Carl sang along with it, particularly loud at the whiney parts.

I loved watching him work. I guess that sounds strange. But he did everything with such, I don't know, joy. He threw his tools up in the air and caught them as he walked around the car. He talked to the car too, almost like it was a drinking buddy of his or something. It was hysterical. I could have watched him for hours.

An old man stepped out of the house and walked across the lawn toward us. He wore baggy boxer shorts and a tank top. He reminded me of Popeye's pappy, only older and more frail. He walked up to Curtis and stood close to him, looking him up and down. "Who the hell are you?" he asked.

"Dad," Carl yelled from the garage. He wiped his hands on a rag as he came toward us.

"You fellows are from the gov'ment, aren't you? Well, if you are, you can get the hell out of here." He pointed toward the highway.

Carl put his hand on his father's shoulder. "Dad, they're just a couple kids I'm paying to help me. They aren't from the government." Carl steered his father away from us.

"Okay," Carl's dad said. "I'm going to keep my eye on you fellows." Carl sat his father down in a rocking chair that sat in the opening of the garage.

"I'm sorry," Carl said. "My father…he's got dementia. He's harmless."

Every time I looked over, Carl's dad was scowling at us. I don't think he blinked even once.

Late in the afternoon, Curtis and I finished loading the truck. Boards, beams, and shingles stuck up over the top of the bed. My arms were sore. My shoulders ached. Curtis and I were covered in dirt except where the sweat made trails down our faces. We were tired and hungry.

Carl was in the garage putting away his tools. His father sat in a rocking chair that creaked as he rocked, and he stared out at the yard.

"Hello," Carl said as we walked into the garage. "Your car is finished."

I took the money out of my wallet and paid him. He thanked me.

"Are there any cheap hotels near here, or a campground?" I shoved my wallet back into my pocket.

Curtis put his hand on the doorway and leaned against it.

"No campgrounds. There's a hotel in town that's not bad. I wouldn't call it cheap, though." Carl held a white rag in his hands and wiped off his tools as he put them away.

"Oh. We don't have much money. We barely have enough to get where we're going."

"Where are you guys heading?" Carl tossed his rag onto his workbench and closed the drawer of his toolbox.

"We've got an uncle up around Memphis. He owns a plumbing business. He told us he'd give us jobs when we got there."

"Memphis?"

"Ever since Mom's boyfriend moved in, it's been pretty hard living there. He drinks a lot." I was laying it on thick. I hated lying to the guy, but there was no way I could tell the truth. "He hit my brother last week." I pointed to Curtis. "That's when we decided it was time to get out of there."

"So you guys are runaways?"

"No sir," I said. "Like I said, we're going to work for my uncle."

"They're okay." His dad turned his head toward us. "They aren't from the gov'ment." He shook his head.

"Yeah?"

"People from the gov'ment don't sweat. These fellows sweat."

"Okay, Dad. Thanks."

He leaned forward in his chair and glared at Carl. "What I mean is, why don't you ask them to stay with us for the night?"

"Oh." Carl paused. "Yeah, I guess, it's the least I can do. I have a spare bedroom." He shrugged at us.

"We don't want to put you out any," I said.

"It's no trouble. I'd enjoy the company. And I'll tell you what—if you need a few extra bucks, tomorrow you can go with me to unload that truck, and there are a few more things that I need to load up and get rid of. I'll pay you each fifty dollars a day."

We grabbed our stuff out of the car and took it into Carl's house. Carl gave us towels to shower with. I took mine first. It had been days since I had really cleaned up. At Skeeter's, showering was another on the list of things that could get done tomorrow.

While Curtis took his shower, I walked around the house. Carl's dad sat in an easy chair in the living room. His hands gripped the armrests as he stared at a blank television screen.

I heard the grinding of an electric can opener through the doorway to the kitchen and the clatter of pots clanging together. I moved my arm through the air to stretch the muscles in my shoulder. They ached from the work I had done. I was tired, but it was a good tired. I felt relaxed. I felt comfortable in Carl's house. It felt like a home there.

A cluster of photos hung on the wall. I shuffled over to take a closer look at them. One was a picture of Carl and his dad standing in front of that garage we tore down, only the garage wasn't that old and neither was Carl's dad. The second was a black-and-white picture of Carl and a woman. A small boy on a tricycle sat between them. The third was of a young man dressed in a cap and gown for high school graduation.

"You sure keep this place neat." I directed my voice to the kitchen doorway.

"I didn't use to." Carl walked into the room with a stack of plates. "When my wife was alive, she was always on me to pick up after myself, but after she died, whenever I saw something lying around out of place, it made me sad, so I was better about putting things away. I guess I thought she could see me from wherever she was and my picking up would make her happy. She'll always be a part of me." The plates thumped to the table, one by one. He went back into the kitchen to stir the beans.

"Is that your son in this picture?" I pointed at the high school picture.

Carl looked out the kitchen doorway. "Yeah, he lives in Washington state the last I heard. We don't talk much anymore. When he turned eighteen, he couldn't hold down a job, and he wouldn't go to school, and he wouldn't join the army. I tried to get him to work with me in the shop, but that didn't work out. He always felt the world owed him something. He came home drunk at all hours. But the worst was that he lied about everything. One thing I can't abide with is a liar. He hooked up with some rich woman from Montgomery, and they took off in a van for Washington State. That was five years ago."

Curtis came out of the bathroom in his jeans, rubbing the back of his head with his towel. He stopped in front of the television. "Man, that shower felt good."

"So your mom's boyfriend was pretty rough on you boys, huh?" Carl came into the dining area with a pot in one hand and a spoon in the other. He walked around the table and spooned beans and franks onto every plate.

"Yeah." Curtis pulled a fresh T-shirt over his head. "He got meaner when he drank. Once, I knocked over his bottle of whiskey. It broke all over the kitchen floor. He put out his cigar against my forearm, right there." He showed Carl the brown circle of scar tissue that Curtis had always said was from brushing his arm against the stove.

"My God!" Carl said. "I don't blame you boys one bit for taking off." His eyes lingered on Curtis, who shrugged his shoulders.

Curtis and I went to bed soon after dinner. We flipped a coin to see who got the bed. I won. Curtis crawled into his sleeping bag on the floor. I slid in between the fresh sheets. It felt so good to be in an actual bed. I hadn't slept in a bed since I left home. I thought about my mom. I hadn't called her or anything since we took off. I knew she was probably going crazy with things the way they were. I decided if I got a chance tomorrow I would call her, if I could sneak away for a bit. She would be at work, but I would leave a message.

A message was best. Talking to her would be too much. She would probably start crying and everything. I didn't want to deal with that.

After Curtis turned off the light, I asked, "How did you really get that burn on your forearm?"

There was silence, long enough that I was sorry I asked. "It was a cigar. My dad did it the day we drove him to the hospital for the last time."

"Why?" I turned to my side and propped my head up with my hand. A light through the bedroom window dimly lit the room, and I was able to make out Curtis's shape through the darkness.

"I don't know. I guess because he knew he was dying, and he had to take it out on someone. I remember him looking at me as he did it, and the look on his face. It was like he hated me. I felt the same toward him at that moment. If I had a gun in my hand, I would've blown him away."

"I don't think anyone would've blamed you. How could he do that to you?"

"Yeah. My old man. There was a meanness in him all right. Sometimes, I could see it. Burning in his eyes. But then…later that day…I mean…he felt bad. Real bad. It was almost like he wanted to cry, but he couldn't." He paused. "He wasn't a man who would ever cry."

"But that doesn't make what he did right."

"No. But he gave me a fifty-dollar bill. He could be so cruel, but then he would be nice as hell, like he had gotten rid of all his pent-up meanness. For a while, anyway. Until it built up in him again. It's hard." Curtis paused again. "Meanness is part of the world. I feel it. I feel it in me. I hate it. I hate seeing it in me. Sometimes I can't stand myself." Curtis rolled away from me. "It doesn't matter. He was dead before that burn on my arm healed. And now that mark is about the only thing that he gave me that I'll always have."

# Moth Nightmares

Early the next morning, Carl drove us to a nearby landfill. He backed up the truck to the edge of a pit. Curtis and I got up on the bed and started grabbing boards and throwing them in as fast as we could. We hadn't been at it very long when Curtis reached into the pile and cried out. He yanked his hand back and held it up. A large splinter stuck out from his palm. It went right through his work glove. It was big, like a spike. I took a step back, gaping at it. I didn't know what to do. It was in pretty deep. Curtis stood there holding his hand in front of his face and staring at it.

Carl climbed up into the truck and went to Curtis. "Hold still, son." He inspected the wound. Carl wrapped his arm around Curtis's and pulled out the splinter. He held it up. The tip was covered with blood.

"Damn, that hurt." Curtis flexed his hand. Blood trickled down his arm.

Carl took off his T-shirt and gave it to Curtis. "Wrap up your hand with this. Why don't you sit in the truck? Jack and I will finish up."

When we got back to Carl's, Carl took Curtis into the garage and got his first-aid kit. Carl put some ointment on the wound and wrapped it up with gauze. He directed us to the backyard. It was filled with discarded appliances, old tires, car parts, and even some furniture. Several old cars, speckled with rust, rested on their frames. "While I'm working in the garage, you boys can load up that truck with as much junk as you can." He clapped his hands. "Let's get cracking." He went toward the cars lined up in front of the garage. He started to whistle.

I put my hand to my mouth, trying to hide a laugh.

He turned toward me. "Do you have a feather in your shorts, son?"

"I've never seen anyone who enjoyed working as much as you do," I said.

Carl put his hands on his hips. "I took over this business from my father about ten years ago. That old garage you boys loaded up onto the truck yesterday?" Carl nodded toward the huge concrete slab that remained. "That was where Daddy did all his work, where he taught me my trade. But that was Daddy's garage." Carl turned to his new garage. "This one is mine. It's taken me years to save up the money to have it built. But I did it."

Curtis moved beside Carl to get a better view of the garage.

"You see that license plate over the garage door." Carl pointed toward an Alabama plate hanging over the double doors. The plate was slightly rusted and one of the corners was bent. "That's from my daddy's car, a 1955 Chevy V-8. He loved his car as much as a man can love anything. I had to sell it last year, after he started losing touch and kept trying to drive it. This year, I still sent in the registration on it. When I got it back, he made me climb up there and put the new sticker on the plate. He spent a lot of time working on that car. Daddy always said that a man should express himself in his work. He worked as long as he was able, and even now, he comes to the garage every day and watches me." Carl nodded.

Curtis and I spent the rest of the morning filling the truck with junk. We worked together to get the appliances loaded. Carl helped us with a refrigerator. When we finished with the appliances, we started on the tires, two at a time. It seemed like there were about a thousand of them. Curtis grimaced every time he grabbed a tire. Carl saw Curtis cradling his hand to his stomach in pain. He walked across the yard toward us.

"Let me see that." Carl took hold of Curtis's hand and unwrapped it. "It's swollen pretty bad." Carl studied the hand closely and gently tested the bones. "I don't think anything is broken."

Curtis gritted his teeth.

"Come on. We need to get it cleaned up and put some ice on it."

Carl took Curtis by the arm and led him into the house. When they returned, Curtis's hand was freshly wrapped, and he held an ice pack on it.

I continued to load the truck. Curtis watched Carl work and asked questions about what he was doing. Carl explained things to him and pointed to different areas in the engine. Curtis nodded. And he was actually smiling too. I don't remember the last time I'd seen him smile. He'd laughed sometimes over the past couple weeks, but in between his laughing, I never saw a smile on his face. And even when he did laugh, it was usually kind of sarcastic, like he was laughing because of how shitty things were.

Curtis got off his stool and helped Carl. He got tools for him and put them away. Curtis seemed to actually enjoy working with Carl. I felt glad for Curtis. He needed something like that.

While they worked in the garage, I made an excuse and went into the house to call Mom. I planned to leave a message on the machine and tell her I was all right and not to worry.

She answered the call on the second ring. "Hello."

I held the phone to my ear and sat there, not knowing what to say, the silence eating into me.

"Hello," she said again.

Still nothing from me.

"Jack?"

"Mom, I want you to know that I'm all right."

"Where are you? Come home. Please."

"I can't. Not yet."

"Don't you know what you're doing to me, Jack?"

I froze. I didn't know what to say. I wished like hell that I hadn't called. I wished like hell she hadn't said what she said. I just wanted to leave a message. I didn't want to deal with it all right then. I didn't want to deal with her.

"Come home."

"Don't worry about me." I disconnected the call with my finger. I looked at the phone for a few minutes and then set it back in its cradle. I should've called her before this. She had always been good to me. Not that I ever let her know that. I knew what this whole thing with Curtis and me must've been doing to her. I mean, she had her boyfriend and everything, but I don't know. I was her kid. She went out of her way for me. I knew that she would always be there for me. I stood there looking at the phone, feeling crappy as hell about the conversation. It was worse than not calling at all, but at least she knew I was all right. That was something, I guess.

In the afternoon, Carl went into town to get some things from the store. Curtis stayed in the garage and wiped off the tools. Once he finished, Curtis came out to help me. A couple smears of grease decorated his cheek. "Carl said we could stay the next couple of days if we wanted to. You know, helping him work around here. He'd pay us."

"That sounds great. We can sure use the money."

"We'd learn a lot too. He showed me all kinds of stuff." There was an excitement in his voice that I hadn't heard in a long time.

When Carl came back, he went straight into the house, carrying a bag of groceries. He walked by like he didn't even see us.

"That was kind of strange," I said.

Curtis stared after Carl. "Yeah, it was."

Carl came out a few minutes later. He waved us over.

We stopped in the doorway of the garage. "I ran into the sheriff in town." Carl stared at the ground. He wouldn't look us in the eye.

Curtis leaned slumped against the doorway of the garage. We both sensed what was coming. Things had caught up with us.

"He asked me if I had seen any runaways. Apparently, they're running because of some incident in Florida. He wouldn't tell me exactly what happened. He thinks they got mixed up with some drug dealers over in Dugan, too." Carl shifted his gaze, directing it at us. I couldn't meet it and glanced down.

"That isn't us." Curtis stiffened and threw his hands out. "We're running away, but we haven't done anything wrong."

"Yeah. Well, one of the drug dealers could draw pretty good, and the drawings I saw fit you guys to a tee." Carl shook his head. "I know you fellows had it pretty rough at home and all, but there're some things I can't abide with. One of them is lying. You need to clear out of here first thing in the morning."

"Did you tell him anything?" Curtis asked.

"I thought it wasn't you," Carl said. Curtis shrank beneath Carl's electric-blue eyes. He looked like the life had been sucked out of him. "No, I didn't say anything to him." Carl took a deep breath. "I don't know what happened back there in Florida. But I can tell you this: you can only run so far and so long before you'll have to face what you did. The sooner you do that, the better off you'll be."

Carl's dad started screaming. He fell from his rocking chair and rolled on the ground, flailing his arms and legs in the air. "Stop them. Stop them."

We rushed over.

"Stop who, Dad?" Carl knelt beside his father.

"The moths." He beat the air in front of his face furiously. "They're all over me. Millions of them. They're on everybody." He looked around wildly. "Get them. Help me!"

"We need to get him into bed." Carl put his hand on his father's chest to hold him steady. "This isn't the first time something like this has happened."

Curtis stepped forward to help.

Carl's dad shrank from Curtis, shaking his head and trembling.

His eyes bulged. "No! Stay away!" He kicked his feet into the ground, trying to push himself back. "The blood. The blood."

Curtis looked at the palms of his hands. Blood had seeped through his bandage, making a small red spot in the center of the gauze covering his hand. Curtis staggered back a step. His mouth dropped open. "I didn't do anything."

"Dad. Dad. It's Curtis. You're fine." Carl gripped his father's shoulders, trying to comfort him. "Curtis, can you go away?" He turned back to me. "Can you help me get him into his room?"

Curtis left. Carl and I each grabbed his father by an arm and lifted him to his feet. We held him between us and walked him into the house. I felt him shuddering, and he wobbled unsteadily. We laid him on his bed.

"I'll go get his medicine." Carl walked out of the room. I sat down on the edge of the bed.

"They're gone now." Carl's dad nodded. He took a deep breath and seemed to relax.

Carl came back. "Here, Dad, take one of these." He put a pill into his mouth and gave him a glass of water.

Carl's dad rolled to his side and curled up against his pillow.

"He's okay now," Carl said.

We went into the living room. Curtis stood in the doorway. Carl saw Curtis, and his expression stiffened "Like I said, you need to pack up and get out of here first thing in the morning." Carl left the room.

"I knew this wouldn't last," Curtis said.

"Curtis, eventually we needed to move on anyway."

"Shut up."

"Man, I'm sorry how things happened. I mean you and Carl. It seemed like you guys were…I don't know—"

"Sorry?" Curtis pouted his mouth and shook his head. "That shit don't mean nothing. I was just doing it for the money. How else am I going to get to Canada?"

The evening passed in silence. Curtis and I stayed in our room.

Just before going to bed, Carl slid an envelope underneath the door. Curtis tore it open. He grabbed the money, gave me half, and stuffed the rest into his pocket. I climbed into the bed.

He hung his head. "I'll never have a real chance." He got on the floor, slid into his sleeping bag, and rolled to his side, his back to me. "I'll never be clean again."

"That's not true." But actually, I felt it was true for him, and for me as well. I turned off the light. I felt like no matter what we did or where we were, we couldn't escape from what happened. I'd temporarily lost sight of the fact that we were running from the law. That was stupid. I felt worse for Curtis than I did for myself. I knew that he was making a connection with Carl, and I knew he needed something like that. He needed it a lot more than I did.

# Elvis Soars

## (Interlude)

Curtis is a moth, flying through the night sky, upward toward the stars. Black markings line his cheeks. His body is fuzzy, bloated at the belly. Two feathery antennas protrude from his forehead and droop down at the tips. His huge brown wings slowly beat the air. I'm flying along beside him and struggle to keep up.

Hundreds of moths flutter along with us through the darkness. The moon appears huge and full. Curtis points to it. Shadows on the surface move like ants and spell out "Graceland." I want to go there. I want to with everything I have. But I feel so tired, and it's still so far. I labor to fly faster, but my wings are heavy and feel like they're moving through water.

Curtis opens his mouth to speak, and a long, thin tongue uncoils from it and penetrates the air. He emits a high-pitched squeal. His expression is worried, etched with strain from trying to flap his wings faster. He bobs down with a jerk. Sandbags are tied to his feet. I feel a yank at my ankles, and see sandbags tied to my feet. We fly at a steep angle to compensate for the extra weight. But we both start to slowly descend. My breathing becomes labored. My energy is being drained away from me.

Elvis comes up behind us. It's Elvis from his Vegas days. He's wearing yellow-lensed sunglasses and a white pantsuit, a cape with silver sequins lining the seams. His hair is bushy, his mutton-chop sideburns distinct. He's pulled up through the sky by wires that attach to his jumpsuit at different points—at his arms and legs, one at the scruff of his neck, one at the seat of his pants. His knees and elbows are bent as he strains to maintain his position. He shifts his weight, trying to gain a better balance, but lurches forward with a twang. He settles into a new position: his face pointing down, his ankles over his head. He grunts in frustration.

"Help us," I say between gasping breaths.

"Help you? You drag me into your dream dangling from these damn wires! You're lucky I don't come up behind you and put my foot up your ass. Believe me, if I could, I would." His weight shifts, and the wires twang again as he's thrown in a new direction. He is now laid out with his arms pointed straight, like Superman in flight. "That's better." Elvis looks up at the moon with Graceland spelled out on it. "There it is, Jack. It's almost within your grasp."

"But I can't make it there. It's too far. I can't fly high enough. My wings are too bulky. The weight around my feet is too much."

"Don't give up now. You're so close."

"So I'll find you at Graceland."

He cocks his head. "I didn't say that, Jack." He presses his lips tight. "Nope. Didn't say that at all. Maybe. Maybe not. No guarantees. I need to tell you something: Before you get to Graceland, you need to save Elvis."

I roll my eyes. "You told me to find Elvis. Now I'm supposed to save him...uh...you."

"You can do both."

"How does that work?"

"The statements aren't mutually exclusive, Jack. It's not exactly rocket science. You can save Elvis and you can find Elvis too. Why's that's so damn confusing?"

"But—"

High-pitched screams from below pierce the night sky, rising and falling in volume. Elvis tilts his head to look down. He adjusts his sunglasses. "That's not good." Hundreds of huge bats flap through the air. They grab moths in their pointy teeth and bite them in half. Some they swallow whole. The bats thrash through the air toward us in a swarm, shrieking as they come.

"You boys might want to renew your efforts."

We continue to slip lower, easing toward the bats below, and the moon shrinks away from us. Fear grips me. It's all slipping from my reach. I stretch my hand up toward it. I want so badly to go there, but it seems impossible.

I look down to Curtis below me. He's gazing up at me. He squeaks in distress.

Elvis nods toward Curtis. He is almost within reach of the bats. "Doesn't look like your friend's doing too well."

The bats' shrieks become louder. They pierce my hearing and vibrate through me. My wings bend against the air from the weight and the stress. I continue to sag lower. The bats are only a few feet below me. I see them nipping at Curtis's feet.

"Can't you help me, Elvis? Please."

Elvis sighs. "Okay, Jack, I'll help you. Come on." He waves for me to follow and ascends toward the moon.

The sandbags drop from my ankles. I begin to soar upward. The sound of a piano rolls through the air. It's "Unchained Melody." Elvis begins to sing. His voice consumes me. I feel the hope within it. I feel joy. Elvis's voice radiates through my soul. He lifts his hands. I rise faster. My wings spread wide and I fly without effort. The moon is huge before me.

Elvis streaks toward it. The music trails after him. He's pulled to the moon and consumed by it, vanishing into the light. I'm not far behind him. His voice comes to me clearly from within the music and the light. "Find me, Jack." His voice echoes from above. "One more thing, Jack. When you get there. If you get there. Look for my pride and joy. That's where you'll find me. That's where I'll be."

"Okay. I will, Elvis. Nothing will stop me."

I'm so close to making it; Graceland is almost within my grasp. Curtis screams from below me. The bats are swooping around him. One clips his wing, and he tumbles in the air. Curtis begins to plummet. Bats swarm on him, biting chunks out of him. I need to save him, but if I turn back now, I know I'll never make it. I have to choose. I look up at the moon. It is huge in front of me. I reach my hand up for it. I can almost touch it. I'm so close, and I want to make it there so badly, but I can't abandon Curtis. I look back to him. He is panicked, shrieking. His arms are stretched out to me. His mouth is open and his eyes are locked onto me. I need to decide . . .

"Wake up!"

• • • • • • • • • • •

"Come on." Curtis shook me. "Wake up. Let's get the hell out of here."

"Okay." The room was pitch black. "What time is it?" I rubbed the back of my head with my hand.

"Who gives a crap? I want to get out of here. Now. Let's go."

We gathered our stuff and slipped out of Carl's house. Curtis got into the driver's seat of his Dart and started the engine. I sat down beside him.

"There's something we need to do before we take off." Curtis unwrapped the bandage from his hand. He flung it out the window, then backed up to the garage. He climbed up on the trunk, reached up, and pried the license plate off.

"Curtis, what're you doing?" I asked.

"You heard Carl. The cops are looking for a car with Florida plates. I'm trying to buy us a little time."

"We shouldn't take it. Carl was good to us."

"Screw him. If he's so nice, why is he booting our asses out of here?"

Curtis removed our plate and replaced it with the Alabama plate. He hopped in our car, and we drove off before the first light came on in the house.

# *Truck Stop*

We headed north. Sunlight beat in through the windshield. The gash on the dashboard pursed up toward it like a swollen eye. Since that first night on the road, when Curtis impaled the picture of the guy fishing in Canada there, the wound had spread open from the heat and tension. It had become a source of dried yellow flecks of foam that dotted the plastic surface and bigger soft chunks that rolled down onto the car seat and the floor.

As Curtis drove, I mapped our path on the atlas to Memphis, to Graceland. It was within our grasp. We had more than enough cash to get there, and if we could somehow make it through an entire day without running into a cop or stumbling into disaster, we would be there tomorrow.

I felt my gut clutch with the thought of it: What then? What would I find when I got there? Would I find anything? Last night's dream cycled through my head. Elvis told me to find his pride and joy, but what would that be? And what had he meant, save Elvis? How was that possible? How could I save him? He was dead. I was a little late, by about four years.

Maybe "Save Elvis" was a clue like the one about the golden arches. It was something that I would understand when it happened, and "Save Elvis" would be just enough so I would know what I needed to do when the time came. That was the only thing that made sense.

But I still struggled to believe the dreams, to believe that Elvis's spirit was communicating with me. It all seemed too fantastic. And maybe I shouldn't believe it. Maybe it was just what it was: a series of dreams. It would've been easy to think that if not for the golden arches clue. That saved us from the cops in Dugan. Because if I hadn't had that clue in my head, I never would've thought about pulling into that McDonald's, and we never would've gotten away; we would've been chased down and arrested then. That was too coincidental for me to discount it. That at least made me consider that there was something at work here. Something more than merely the inner workings of my mind. There was something at a deeper, I don't know, spiritual level. I wanted to believe that, anyway, and I needed to know for sure.

And I was sure if we made it to Graceland, I would either get the proof or not. Either way, that would give me with the answer I needed. Nothing was going to stop me from going there.

But after that, what? Would I go on, onward to Canada? At some point I had to face things. I couldn't run forever. Facing things meant getting arrested, meant potential jail time. That was a scary thought. Maybe it wouldn't be as bad as I thought. Maybe we weren't in as much trouble as I feared.

"I wonder what happened to Bruce when he got home." I noticed the crumpled magazine cover by my feet. The edge of it, creased and torn, stuck out from under my seat.

Curtis looked at me smartly. "We can ask the next cop we come across. Maybe he could find out for us." Curtis hadn't had anything positive to say since we left Carl's.

"We could call him."

Curtis scrunched his face like he had taken a bite of a lemon.

"No." He tightened his grip and tensed in his seat. "I don't want to talk to his sorry ass."

"He would know what was going on by now."

"Yeah." Curtis paused then shook his head. "He'll rat on us."

"Yeah, he would. If it would help him." I looked ahead and pressed my lips together. "I'll lie. I'll tell him we're almost to Canada."

"Yeah," Curtis nodded. "Maybe that's not a bad idea."

But there was more to calling Bruce than finding out what happened with the old man and what happened to Bruce when he got back. Part of me missed home, missed the life I had there. Missed my mom. Especially after that shitty phone call I had with her. Even though when I was living there with her, I hated it, and all I talked about was how it sucked and how I couldn't wait to get out on my own. I missed it. Not so much for what it was but for what I wished it could've been. And I wanted to touch it in some way, make sure that it was all still there, that it hadn't changed. Even though I knew it had; I knew the life we left wasn't there for us anymore. Not really. Even if we did go back, it would never be the same, not for us. We had seen to that.

Curtis got off the interstate at the next exit and pulled into a truck stop. Tractor-trailers growled through the parking lot past the diesel pumps. A phone booth sat next to a lamppost. Curtis angled the car in front of the booth.

I poked through the ashtray where we dumped all of our loose change. Motor oil had spilled into it, so all the coins were coated. They were pretty nasty. I scrounged through them, scooping up anything silver. There was plenty. When I was done, I cupped my hands together to hold it all and went into the booth.

I leaned back, holding the change with one hand against my shirt while I used my other hand to try to close the folding door. It stuck in its runners, and it took a few attempts before I could scrape it shut. A couple of coins clattered to the metal floor.

I dialed Bruce's number. I decided if either of his parents answered, I would hang up. I was told I needed to deposit $4.75 for the call to be put through. I filled the slot. My hands had gotten oily, and handling the slippery coins was hard. Some slid from my fingers and clanged to the ground. I didn't bother with them. I kept shoveling in change until the call went through.

"Hello," Bruce said.

"Hey." I held the handpiece to my ear with one hand, and with the other, I gripped the spiral-ridged metal cable that connected it to the phone.

"Jack?"

"Yeah." I slid my fingers idly along the cable, clicking my fingernail over the ridges. I wasn't sure how to begin.

"Where are you?"

I ignored his question. "What's going on?" I asked, like I was calling him on a Saturday morning when we were back in school.

"I'll tell you what's going on." Anger swelled in his voice as he spoke. "I got arrested for the crap you and Curtis pulled. I'm going to court next month and maybe to jail because of your sorry asses. That's what's going on. You jerks got me into big time trouble."

"Sorry."

"Sorry? Is that all you can say? You guys need to get your butts back here and take the blame for this shit."

"I don't think we can help you out there." I looked above the pay phone. Phone numbers and names were etched into the metal frame. Black fingerprints smudged the white plastic of the booth.

"Where the hell are you anyway?"

"We're twenty miles from the Canadian border."

"Canada? That's got Curtis written all over it. That's nuts. I don't know why you listen to that—"

I didn't want to hear it. "What happened with the old guy?" I wrapped my index finger around the stiff cable. "Is he okay?" The odor of spent diesel fuel filled the booth. It made me nauseous. I held my breath, waiting for the answer.

"I don't know about okay, but he's not dead. Last I heard anyway. He's got problems, though. He'll be drinking his meals for a while.

His guts are all torn up. But they say he's going to make it."

I leaned back against the glass wall and exhaled. At least we weren't murderers. "That's a relief."

"A relief? That guy has been fucked up for life, maybe. Is that all you can say about it?"

"What do you want me to say?"

"How about, 'My God, that's awful,' 'I wish every day that I could take it back,' 'Please, dear God, forgive us.'"

"If it'll make you feel better, I'll say that. But how's that going to change anything?"

"Well, you need to think about someone besides yourselves."

"You mean think about you?"

"That's right. Think about me. I didn't have anything to do with what happened, and you know it."

"Yeah. When did they catch up to you?"

"It took about two days. They had Curtis's license plate number, so they started with his mom, but, when everybody figured out he wasn't turning up, they came to me. Man, what a—" A truck roared by. Puffs of white smoke shot from the exhaust pipe at the top of the cab as it passed. "—hold out for you guys, but that lady came down and identified me, and they had me cold. What an acid scene that was. My mom totally freaked. I held it together pretty good under their bright, hot lights and long rubber hoses."

"Uh huh." I could imagine how well Bruce held up. If one end of the holding up spectrum was James Cagney in *White Heat* and the other was Oliver Hardy crying like a baby, I was pretty sure I knew which end Bruce was closest to.

"I told them the whole story. I told them everything. How you and Curtis broke into the trailer and how Curtis shot that guy."

"What a pal."

"Hey, you know it's true."

He did have me there.

"Calling me a pal. I'm the one stuck holding the bag. You guys are out there on one of Curtis's crazy joy rides."

"Joy ride? We're just trying to stay out of trouble and somehow keep going."

"Good luck staying out of trouble with Curtis. I've seen your mom a few times since I got back. She's pretty busted up about everything. I guess she never imagined that her son would end up as an accomplice to an armed assault. You haven't even called her, have you?"

I thumped my head against the wall and closed my eyes at the thought of that short talk I'd had with her at Carl's. That was worse than not calling her. I said nothing to Bruce about it.

"Even Curtis's mom is all broken up about him. I guess he's all she's got in this world, since Curtis's dad died. How is Curtis, anyway? Is he still borderline psycho?"

"Curtis is fine!"

"Is that what you tell yourself, Jack? I don't know about you, but I've done a lot of thinking about that day. Curtis had lost it, man. If you hadn't stopped him, he would've been coldblooded. You know that. You saw that look in his eyes. You know what he was thinking about doing. He would've—"

I used my index finger and disconnected the call. I leaned my head against the phone. The dial tone buzzed in my ear. I gritted my teeth. I remembered that look on Curtis's face. That look was etched into my head. It was a wild look, like a cornered dog. I didn't know what he was going to do. I told myself that Curtis wouldn't have gone through with it. I told myself he would've stopped himself. But there was no doubt about what he was thinking about doing and that was one scary true fact. But thinking about doing something and actually doing it are two different things. Besides, that was a pretty intense scene. A lot of things ran through my mind. But I couldn't shake the reality that I was on the road with him. What would he do if we got into a situation like that again? And would I be able to stop him the next time?

I grabbed the cable in my fist and yanked down on it. The thick cable vibrated to a stop. I slapped the phone into its cradle and went to the car. Curtis's head was tilted back against the headrest. His eyes were shut, and his mouth open. I thought he was about to start snoring.

"Wake up."

Curtis lifted his head and looked at me, annoyed. He placed his hands on the wheel and pushed back into his seat, stretching. Then he rubbed his eyes with his palms and ran his fingers through his thick hair. "So. How was Mr. Wonderful?"

I told Curtis everything Bruce had said except for the last part. The whole time I was talking he kept his head leaned back against the headrest and his eyes closed. Occasionally, he nodded.

When I finished, Curtis lifted his head. "At least the old guy made it."

The magazine cover that Curtis had nailed to the dash that first day poked out from under my seat. I reached down and picked it up. The knife fell from it and landed on the floor. I picked up both the picture and the knife.

Curtis reached out for it. "Give me that," he said. I turned the handle toward him and he took the knife, folding it shut and shoving it in his pocket.

I studied Curtis. I smoothed out the picture as best I could, but it was creased and had a big gash in the center. I held it out for Curtis. "Do you want this?"

"Nah, it's all messed up. Let's go and eat."

I balled up the picture. "Yeah. I'm starved."

Curtis drove across the parking lot to the truck stop. I got out of the car and flung the heavy door closed. The broken glass inside crunched. I shoved the magazine cover into a trashcan as we entered the truck stop diner.

# **Another Curtis**

Curtis and I sat at a booth along the window. Large trucks lumbered through the parking lot, growling over the patter of conversation. I pulled two menus from between a container of sugar packets and two plastic bottles: mustard and catsup. I handed a menu to Curtis.

The waitress came to take our order. She looked old for her age; I could tell she was young, but the skin on her face seemed worn, weathered. She had the vacant eyes of someone who had spent too many years doing something she never planned on doing in the first place and who knew she would be doing it a lot longer. I don't know why I thought that. But that was how she struck me. I ordered a burger, Curtis, a chicken sandwich.

A girl came in and sat down a couple booths behind Curtis. She was tall and thin, with shiny auburn hair held together on one side by a barrette. I sat up and took a closer look at her. It was the girl from the store the other night. Becky. She set her backpack on the seat beside her and slid into the booth, her back to us.

I grabbed Curtis by the wrist. "It's that girl! From a couple nights back. At the store."

Curtis turned around in his seat. "Are you sure?"

I paused for a minute.

She looked to the side.

"Positive. Come on. I want to talk to her." I got up.

Curtis slid out of the booth and followed. "Yeah, I've got a few things I want to say to her too."

She was rummaging through her pack as we walked up. "Damn," she said. She tossed a couple of crumpled dollar bills onto the table. She glanced at us, then continued going through her bag. "Can I help you?"

Curtis thumped his hands on the table and looked down at her. "Do you remember us?"

She leaned back and folded her arms across her chest and appraised Curtis. "You do look kind of familiar." She looked at me. "Oh yeah. I remember you." She nodded and smiled. "I knew you would help me. You have that look about you."

I smiled back at her. Curtis scowled.

"So how's it going?" she asked me.

"It's—"

"How's it going? We barely got out of there before the cops showed up that night thanks to your lame ass and your stupid boyfriend."

"Curtis, leave it alone. That's not her fault."

She cocked her head to the side and smacked her tongue. "That guy wasn't my boyfriend." Her long, shiny hair swung across her shoulders. "He was just some guy that was giving me a ride."

"I bet."

She turned away and resumed digging through her pack. "Eddie was harmless. I just needed to get away from him." She paused and looked us over. "You guys don't look like you suffered too badly from the experience."

"Didn't suffer—"

"No, we got out of it unscathed." I pushed my way in front of Curtis. "So do you mind if we join you?"

She shrugged. "Why not?"

"Join her. We ought to—"

"Curtis, forget it. It wasn't that big a deal." I slid into the booth across from her. Curtis slid in beside me.

"I'm Jack, and this is Curtis."

"Hello. So where are you guys heading?"

"We have an uncle up around Memphis. We're going there," I said. "Where are you headed?"

She turned to me and lifted her chin. "California. Hollywood. I've got a cousin out there. She's going to let me stay with her." She talked with a lot of energy. Her face and head were in constant motion. I liked that about her. "She's near the beach. I love the ocean. It's all set up for me. She works at a mall there and says she can get me—"

"What do you want?" the waitress broke in.

Becky jumped. "Ah…chicken soup."

"Don't have it." The waitress impatiently tapped her pencil on her order pad. "Clam chowder or vegetable."

"I'll have a cup of vegetable soup."

The waitress wrote down her order and walked off.

"What are you going to Hollywood for?" I asked.

"I don't know. See what it's like. It's a place I want to go. For now. I'm not sure what I'll do there. If I like it, I'll probably get a job. Maybe I'll be an actress."

Curtis laughed. "Isn't that what everyone who goes out there says they're going to do?"

"Yeah, I guess." Her face scrunched. "So what? That doesn't mean I can't. I can be an actress if I want to. I'd be good at it."

Curtis shook his head. "You've got to be beautiful to be in movies. You aren't that hot."

"Well, thank you for the compliment." Her eyes narrowed as she looked at Curtis, then back to me. "But I'll go out there anyway. Who knows what'll happen." Her attention shifted back to Curtis. She leaned back and laid her arm along the top of the seat. "But I'd be a good actress. I was in drama in high school. I played Rizzo in *Grease*. The director said he would give me the lead next year, but I bailed on drama."

"I apologize. I'm sure with your vast acting experience you'll be in high demand," Curtis said. I wanted to tell Curtis to shut up. I liked this girl. Maybe he saw her as an outlet for all his anger and frustration. Maybe he wanted to wreck any chance I had with her. Maybe meanness was all that was left in him.

"I am good," Becky said. Her eyes didn't move from Curtis.

Curtis rolled his eyes and nodded.

"Why don't you show us how good you are?" I asked.

"I don't know," she said.

"I'd like to see you act."

"I guess I could." She looked at Curtis. "To prove you wrong." She straightened, closed her eyes, and took a couple of deep breaths.

"What are you doing?" Curtis leaned back against his seat.

She opened one eye. "I'm getting myself in the mood, you bonehead."

She put the back of her hand to her forehead and started acting like Scarlet O'Hara from *Gone with Wind*. She talked about Rhett and Ashley and Tara. She was pretty good, but I don't remember Scarlet calling Rhett a dumbass like Becky did.

When she finished, I applauded. Curtis looked away. "She was pretty good. Wasn't she?" I asked him.

"I guess so," he said.

After our meal, I dropped a couple bucks on the table for a tip and headed to the register to pay. Becky made an excuse to go back to the table, saying she had forgotten something. I watched her pick up the tip money and slide it into her pocket. I stepped out the door and waited for her.

She busted out the door and blew past me. "Good bye," she said over her shoulder as she headed across the parking lot.

"Do you want to ride with us to Memphis? That's kind of in your direction." I said. "You can head west from there." I felt Curtis glaring at me, but I didn't care. I hoped she would come with us. I wanted to help her. I thought maybe she could use a little help. And I wanted to hang out with her some more. She was a free spirit and I liked that about her. I liked that she was heading out to California. Just following her heart and seeing what happened.

She stopped, turned, and took a couple steps back in our direction. "I guess so, if your friend doesn't mind."

I looked at Curtis.

"I'm thrilled," Curtis said.

Becky threw her pack on top of our cooler and got in beside it.

Curtis got back on the interstate. Becky stretched out across the backseat and leaned against the cooler. Curtis rolled down his window. Air blasted through the back of the car. Becky's barrette waved like a kite tail in the air, and her loose hair flapped wildly.

"Could you roll up your windows?" She squinted from the wind blasting against her face.

"I can't. Mine's broken," I said.

Curtis looked at her in the rear-view mirror. "I like the air rushing through the car. It makes me feel like I'm getting some place."

"Where are you going? Jerkville?" Becky ran her hand across the side of her face to hold back some of her flapping hair.

"Yeah, do you want me to drop you off at Bitch City?" I came to understand that the two of them just didn't and wouldn't ever get along. It was like putting a mongoose in a closet with a cobra. You know a battle to the death will follow. All I could do was try to keep them from killing each other.

"Curtis, roll it up a little," I said. He closed it about halfway.

As we headed north, Becky closed her eyes and slowly slipped lower and lower on the seat until her soft snores gave a pulse to the car. It was getting late in the day. We were four hours from Memphis, and we wouldn't make it there that day. I suggested that we start looking for a campground. Curtis wanted to ditch Becky when she got up, but I told him no.

"You got the hots for her?" he asked.

I didn't say anything.

"You do." He shook his head. "That girl's trouble. If she gets the chance, she'll screw us over."

After Becky woke up, I asked her if she wanted to share a campsite. She thought that was a good idea. Curtis added that it would give her a good rest before she set out west to Hollywood on her own tomorrow.

We found a campground north of Tupelo. The campground was nearly empty. Our site had two picnic tables set side by side in front of a barbecue grill. Scraggly pine trees formed a border between our site and the vacant sites around us.

We unloaded our stuff. I pulled out our lantern, and Curtis tossed his sleeping bag onto one of the picnic tables. Becky untied her sleeping bag from the bottom of her pack and set it on the other table. She started to empty her bag. It was filled mostly with clothes. She pulled out an old, worn blanket with pictures of ballerinas across it. As she threw it on the table, it unrolled, and a stuffed cow fell out. She went after it.

Curtis snatched it up. "What the hell is that?"

"That's nothing." She reached out, trying to grab it back.

Curtis kept it away from her. "Isn't that sweet." He tilted his head to the side sarcastically. "She's got a little stuffed animal."

"Give me that, you jerk." She reached around him to try to get it. He held it over her head.

"Holy crap, Curtis. Give her the damn cow!"

He tossed it to her and announced he'd be going for a walk. I was glad.

"Take your time," Becky said.

He scowled back at us as he walked away.

Becky and I sat on top of one of the picnic tables in our campsite and talked. When it got dark, I lit our Coleman lantern. Becky was from Langston, a small town south of Atlanta, and her mom worked at the high school cafeteria. She left home right after she graduated from high school and had been hopping from place to place for the last year.

"What does your father do?" I asked. In the light of the lantern, the shadow of Becky's nose stretched across her cheek. Her elbows rested on her knees and her feet, on the bench of the table.

"He's a trucker. That's why I don't feel scared about hitchhiking."

"Where did you go after you left Langston?"

"I had a friend up around New York, and I went and lived with him for a while, till I found out about his other girlfriend." She idly stroked her hand through her long hair. "I packed up my bag, and headed south. I went down to Miami for a couple months, then I hitched down to Key West. That's when I called my cousin. I've been heading west ever since."

"You ever talk to your parents?"

"I drop them a postcard every now and then. Let them know I'm alive, but that's it. I wouldn't know what to say." She spoke softly.

"Why did you leave home?" I slid a bit closer to her.

"I don't know. I got bored, I guess. I knew there was something I wanted, somewhere, but I wasn't sure what it was or where it was. Right now, it seems like it's in Hollywood. Who knows?" She shrugged her shoulders then looked at me. "I'm seeing the world, anyway. What about you? Where are you guys heading?"

"We're headed to Graceland."

"What for?"

"I'm a big Elvis fan. Curtis is too. I love him. I want to see where he lived. I want to see where he's buried. Just to see it, I guess." I paused and shook my head. No way I could tell her all of it. "I don't know. It's some place to go. Everybody's looking for something."

"What about after that?"

"Curtis wants us to keep going north to Canada. To get out of the country. To get away from things."

"Get away from things?"

"We got in a little trouble." I bit the inside of my cheek. "Actually, we got into a lot of trouble. The cops are after us."

She tilted her head like she was asking me to tell her more about it, but I didn't. "Well, whatever you guys did, you're going to have to face it eventually. Besides, you shouldn't run away from things."

"I'm not running away." I thought for a moment. "Maybe I am, kind of."

"If you stay on the road long enough, all that will be left is running. Once you start, it's hard to stop. It becomes hard to settle in any one place. Believe me. I know." She leaned in closer until her hand was almost touching my knee.

I looked at her, noticing her soft brown eyes. "I'm glad we ran into you again. It's been nice having someone else to talk to. It's only been the two of us for the last couple weeks."

"I can imagine what that's like."

I laughed. "Curtis isn't bad."

"Not bad? Compared to what?"

I laughed again. "Maybe the two of you are too much alike."

"That's a scary thought." She leaned back and yawned. "I'm getting sleepy." She got up and unrolled her sleeping bag on the picnic table behind us.

I twisted my body around on the table and lay on my back.

"You don't have a sleeping bag?" I heard her slide into her bag.

"I had to leave it behind."

"Do you want to share mine?"

"Okay." I turned off the lantern and went over to her. She held the flap up, and I slid my legs down into the sleeping bag next to hers. We lay face to face. She put her arms around me. I zipped the bag tight around us. Our bodies pressed together. I kissed her and held her as tight as I could and kissed her some more. It was nice holding her and kissing her like I did, but that was all we did. It takes me a while to warm up to a girl, to want to do more than that, even though I liked her. I don't think she would've let me anyway. But still, it was nice sleeping with her, to smell her and to feel her next to me. Feeling her breath against my chest, I closed my eyes and lay there for the longest time until I drifted off.

# No Good Deed

The next morning, Curtis sat on the picnic table across from Becky and me, pine nuts cupped in his hand. Several lay by my head. "Rise and shine, lovebirds." He threw another. It bounced off my forehead.

"Hey!" I rubbed my head.

Becky groaned.

"Come on, sunshine." Curtis tossed one at Becky. "You're not a Hollywood movie star yet."

Becky raised her arm behind her, middle finger extended.

We pulled our stuff together. I wrote my name and address on a piece of paper and took sixty dollars out of my wallet. I wrapped the paper around the money and stuck it in her pack. That was about all I had, except for a twenty. I didn't tell Curtis. He'd be pissed if he knew I gave her all my money. I told Becky I wanted her to write when she got settled. She said that she would. I didn't tell her about the money.

The morning was hot; vapor rippled up from the pavement ahead of us. I drove, and Curtis rode shotgun. Becky sat in the back.

We had been on the road about an hour when we saw two vehicles pulled over on the outside lane. The first was a small white car with its flashers on and the hood up. The other car was an old, sky-blue Ford pickup, stopped about twenty yards ahead of the first car.

"Oh my gosh," I said. "It's Elvis." Like an alarm bell, "Save Elvis" rang in my head. My hands tensed on the steering wheel. This was what I had been warned about in my dream. This was going to be my chance to "Save Elvis." It had to be.

"Let's blow by," Curtis said. "He doesn't need our help."

"No, I'm stopping." Driving by was not a choice. I had to know for sure. I slowed down and edged off onto the shoulder. Becky and I got out and went toward the scene. Cars and trucks rushed by. When there was a break in the traffic, Curtis hopped out and headed after us.

Elvis stood under the open hood of the white car, looking at the engine. His peach jacket was draped over the side of his pickup. He straightened and wiped sweat off the back of his neck with his handkerchief. A patch of sweat made an oval in the center of his back. A truck blasted by. Hot air swirled around us.

A woman stood beside him. She used her arms to hold down the dress that fit her like a tent. She divided her time between watching Elvis and keeping an eye on her two boys. They chased each other around below us on the median that sloped steeply like a trough between the north and the southbound traffic.

"Do you need any help?" I asked.

Elvis turned toward us and then smiled. "I remember you fellows." Sweat ran in lines down his face. "I don't think so. Looks like her engine overheated. Like it's not hot enough without sticking my face under that hood."

Curtis stopped behind us and put his hands on his hips. Becky poked her head forward to look at the engine. The air radiated heat and smelled of car exhaust.

The two boys, around the ages of seven and ten, wrestled with each other on the grass. The younger boy broke free from his brother and ran around his mother into the back of Elvis, who staggered back a step toward the road.

I jumped forward and grabbed his elbow to steady him. "Watch yourself," I said.

"You boys settle down," the lady said to them. She might as well have been telling her pet rock to jump. One of the boys threw the other on the ground and put him in a headlock. They tumbled around, cursing and threatening each other.

"What a couple of rambunctious youngsters." Elvis laughed pleasantly to the woman.

"Do you think that you can fix it?" the woman asked.

Elvis turned his attention back to her car. "Yeah, I got the hose hooked up again." He tromped around the front of the car, testing the connection at both ends. His too-large boots huffed air with every step. "We need to let it cool and then get some water into the radiator."

The woman had a blank look on her face. She kept her focus on her kids. The smaller boy had wriggled out of the headlock and ran circles around his mom to keep away from the bigger boy. "Can't catch me. Can't catch me," he yelled.

"Stop that, boys," she said.

"Do you have any water?" he asked me.

I turned to Curtis. He was leaning against Elvis's truck. "Do we have any water in the car?" I asked.

Curtis shrugged.

"I think there's some in your cooler." Becky headed to our car. "I'll get it."

"J.J., stop that," the large lady said.

"Watch out, son!" Elvis yelled.

A kid yelped. I turned. The younger boy had fallen into the middle of the outside lane. A van headed toward him. Terror washed over his face. He screamed. I stood there frozen while the van bore down on him. Elvis brushed past me into the road, grabbed the boy, and threw him to the side. The little boy sprawled across the median grass, tumbling down the slope. The van screeched, skidding toward Elvis. The back wheels fishtailed slightly. He attempted to run out of the way, but, on his first step, his foot pulled up inside his boot. When he tried to go forward, the boot bent over, and he stumbled over it. He found his balance and stood up straight. But it was too late. His face tightened with resolve before the impact. I'll never forget the sound, like a wet towel thrown hard against a cement wall. He slid past me across the median grass and down the slope on his back like an inverted bobsledder. He came to a rest at the bottom. His socks were half off and drooped limply over the top of his feet.

"Curtis!" I screamed. I ran down the median to Elvis.

I stood over him, lost for what to do. He lay in the grass. His arm was twisted underneath his body. His leg was bent unnaturally behind him. His head lay at an odd angle. He looked like a broken puppet. I knelt beside him, afraid to touch him. I was stunned, overcome with guilt and shock.

Curtis stood at the top of the median with his arms at his side, shaking his head dumbly back and forth. Becky made her way down the slope and stopped behind me.

Elvis tried to lift himself but only winced in pain. "Is the boy all right?" he asked.

The mother held the boy in her arms while he bawled.

"Yeah, he's okay," I said.

"Good." A spasm gripped Elvis. He reached up and grabbed my shirt. "Oh God, that hurts. I'm all broken up inside."

"Don't move," I said. "We'll get you some help."

Curtis shifted back and forth on his feet. He looked like he was about to cry. I felt Becky's hand on my back.

Elvis put one hand on my shirt. "Don't leave me." With the other hand, he reached into his pocket and pulled something out. He gripped it tightly. I couldn't make out what it was. I saw glints of white and black in the gaps between his fingers. "Oh God." His body contorted in pain. Clutching the object, his hand thumped to his chest. A drop of blood rolled from the corner of his mouth down to his chin and hung there.

Becky knelt on the other side of him. She put her hand gently on his forehead.

Curtis jogged down the bank and stopped behind me.

Elvis coughed. A light spray of blood burst from his mouth and dotted his white shirt and tie. "There was never enough time." His fingers shook as they rolled back and showed the small ivory statue he held. He reached out toward me. "Take this." He placed the statue into my hand. His entire body shuddered. He clutched at my shirt. "D-d-d-on't . . ." As if with an audible click, the light in his eyes went out. His head turned to the side, and his dead eyes stared blankly at the passing traffic, a half smile frozen on his face.

"Can't we help him?" Curtis put his hand to his mouth, pinching his upper lip. He was trembling. "Isn't there something we can do?"

Bowing her head, Becky cupped her face in her hands.

I knelt on the grass and slumped my head. I felt like I had been slammed in the gut with a sledgehammer.

Curtis and Becky looked at me as if they were both waiting for me to say something, to make some pronouncement. But I didn't want to say it, to say what each of us knew. Saying it would make it all real, saying it would make it all hurt even more, but whether I said it or not that didn't change that it was real, that it did happen.

And I had been warned. I had known something was going to happen, but, in the moment, I froze. I did nothing. I didn't do what I was meant to do. All I did was watch. If I had gone after the kid, I would've had time to save him and get out of the way, and I wouldn't've had boots to trip over. But in that moment, I hesitated. And it was all too late now. I could never take it back.

The driver of the van appeared at the top of the bank. "Is he hurt bad?" he called down to us.

"No. He's dead." I said it like I was throwing a rock at the guy.

He started shaking visibly. "He…he jumped out in front of me. I…I…couldn't do anything. First, the kid ran out, then that man grabbed the kid and threw him out of the way, then…then…it was too late."

I looked at the small ivory statue I held in my hand. The face of the statue was painted, but the rest of it was pure white. At first, I thought it was a statue of Jesus. The figure wore long robes like Jesus and had long flowing hair and held a cross, but when I looked closer, I saw sideburns painted evenly on his face, the top of his hair styled in a pompadour. He held something in front of his face. At first I thought it was a cross, but it was a microphone. Electric blue dots covered the eyes, and his mouth was shaped into a snarl. It was a statue of Elvis, or maybe it was Elvis Christ.

Curtis looked at the statue in my hand. "We need to get out of here before the cops and ambulance get here."

"He's right," Becky said. "When the cops get here they're going to want to talk to everyone. They'll nail you guys."

I slid the statue into my pocket. "We can't leave him like that."

"There are other people here. They can take care of him," Curtis said.

The woman and the man had stupid looks on their faces. They had no idea what to do. Both the boys were clutching at their mother's leg.

"No, they don't even know him."

"We don't know him either," Curtis said.

"I know." I said. "I just can't leave him like this. It's all my fault."

"How is it your fault?" Curtis asked.

"I can at least cover him."

I ran back to the car and opened the trunk to see if we had anything to lay over him, a blanket, a towel, anything. There was nothing. I reached into my pack and yanked out one of my T-shirts. I ran back down the bank to Elvis and laid it over his face.

A cop car pulled off next to us. Two cops got out and headed toward us.

"Crap," Curtis said.

I felt relieved and wanted it to end here. I didn't want to go on. Not after what happened.

"You guys make an excuse to get back to your car and keep going," Becky whispered to us. "I'll do something to distract them."

I tilted my head at her. "Keep going?"

Curtis grabbed me by the arm. "Yeah, come on. We can still get out of this. We can't give up."

"I don't know." I looked at the ground. I couldn't shake the thought that it was my fault he was dead. I didn't deserve to go on from here. I stood there in a daze.

Curtis grabbed me by the shoulder and shook me. "Come on. Snap out of it! There's nothing we can do for him now. We have to get out of here."

I took a deep breath and nodded.

Two cops got out and made their way toward us. "What happened here?" one asked, looking down the bank at us. He was a pudgy cop. With his right hand, he hiked his sagging belt up.

The man who hit Elvis looked like he was about to wet himself. "That fellow jumped out in front of me. I didn't have any choice. There was nothing I could do." He pointed down the slope to where Elvis lay. He didn't give a crap that he had killed someone. All he cared about was getting out of trouble.

The other cop, who was tall and thin and younger than his partner, stood next to the van driver. "That man's dead?" he asked. The cops made their way down the bank.

"What was he doing in the road?" the pudgy cop asked.

"One of those kids ran into the highway," Curtis said. "And Elvis...I mean, this guy here threw the kid out of the way."

"He saved the kid's life," Becky said.

"Elvis?" The tall cop placed his hand idly on the top of his nightstick.

"That's what we called him," I said. "He looked a lot like Elvis."

"What was his real name?" the pudgy cop asked.

"I don't know," I said.

The cop nodded and told his partner to search him for ID. "We'll need to check his truck." He turned to us. "I'm going to need to see some ID's from everyone."

"My wallet's in our car," Curtis said. "Do you want me to go get it?"

The cop nodded.

I followed after him.

"Where are you going?" the cop asked me.

"My ID's in the car, too."

He nodded.

Becky fanned herself. "I do declare. It's powerfully hot today, I must say." I looked back at her as we walked away. She winked at me. I wasn't sure if I would ever see her again. I hoped I would. At least, I hoped that she would find my note in her pack and write to me. Maybe somehow we could stay connected. Maybe we would see each other again. Some day. When all this was over. But as I walked back to our car, that didn't seem likely. We were headed in two different directions.

Nothing needed to be said between me and Curtis. I got in on the driver's side, and Curtis got in beside me. Looking in the rear-view mirror, I saw Becky faint directly into the arms of the pudgy cop. The cop lowered her gently to the ground. Both cops huddled over her as she lay on the ground with the back of her hand across her forehead.

I started the car. Becky grabbed the tall cop by the shirt and started shaking like she was having some kind of a seizure. I popped it into drive and rolled forward. Something in the road caught my eye. Elvis's boots stood in the middle of the freeway, heels together and toes pointed slightly out, as if they had been set there, side by side, facing the oncoming traffic.

Curtis noticed the boots too. "Let's get out of here." He looked the other way with a pained expression on his face. "Don't mean nothing."

"That shit," I said almost in a whisper.

I drove off. An ambulance about a mile back parted the traffic, rushing toward the scene that shrank behind us.

"I can't believe that guy. Why did he save that kid? Why did he give himself up like that?" Curtis sounded like he was mad at Elvis.

"I don't know."

Curtis shook his head. "He screwed up. He thought he could save himself and the kid, but he couldn't. If he had it to do over again, he would've let that kid get creamed."

So what if Elvis thought he could save himself too? He still put himself out there. He gave his life to save that kid. That was more than I did. More than Curtis did. I didn't think Elvis could move that fast. He jumped out there without hesitation, without a thought to himself. And maybe it was one of those things that you don't even think about doing; you just do it. But if he had the chance to do it over again, he would've done the same thing. I knew that from the look on his face. As he straightened before the oncoming van, he was resigned to the choice he made. He had no regret. And the first thing he did after he got hit was ask about that kid. He died knowing he had sacrificed himself for someone else. I didn't think that I could ever do anything like that.

Curtis looked out his window; the corners of his mouth pointed down like a bulldog. He muttered to himself. "Don't mean nothing. Don't mean nothing."

I pulled the statue out of my pocket. The base was heavy, weighted. I set it on the dashboard above the yellow gash, pursed like a sideways eye or an open sore. The electric blue eyes of the statue burned straight ahead. With its arm raised and microphone to its mouth, the statue perched above the gash that spread up before it in the sweltering heat as if bearing witness to the final unfolding of a withering flower.

# 3764 Elvis Presley Boulevard

"Memphis City Limits" gleamed from the emerald sign along the freeway. Curtis looked to me and smiled. We had made it. We got off the interstate and stopped at a gas station for directions to Graceland. The attendant seemed to know where we were going before we even asked. From there, it was a short drive to Elvis Presley Boulevard.

We parked at a strip mall near the front gate. Tacky Elvis signs hung across the fronts of many of the stores proclaiming great deals on Elvis souvenirs. We walked through one store. Novelties and gifts sat in bins lining the counters. The signs above the bins read: "Two for a dollar" or "Buy one get one half off." I picked up an Elvis key ring and looked at it. It was the same kind that Elvis guy sold out of his steamer trunk. It made me think about him, lying there on the side of the road, with blood leaking from the side of his mouth, dead. I squeezed it in my fist, then dropped it back in the bin with all the others. I hoped that Becky was back on the road by now, and I guessed that she was. They wouldn't have any reason to hold her.

We left the store and headed up the street toward the mansion. In the muggy air, gnats danced around my eyes and hair. I kept swiping them away. Clouds had rolled in and provided cover from the sun, but the air was hot like a steamy bathroom.

The gates stood shut. I went up to one, wrapped my fingers around the metal, and peered through. Standing on the asphalt driveway next to a brick guard shack, a guard flapped his wide-brimmed hat to cool himself.

Each white wire gate contained an image of a man leaned back, holding a guitar with musical notes floating off the end of it. The notes seemed to float across white bars, wavy like sheet music. The driveway ran from the gate, curved out of sight behind a knoll, and arrived at the mansion that was set back behind a sparse patch of trees. At the bottom of the mansion steps, a white statue of a lion perched on each side. The house seemed smaller than I imagined.

I had heard that every day since Elvis died, people could walk around on the grounds and could even walk back to his grave and pay their respects. But not the day we came. The day we came the gates were closed and locked. Just our luck.

I stepped away from the gate and put my hand on one of the columns, feeling the coarse brick with my fingertips. I wasn't sure what I should be looking for. I expected some sign or something that would give me some indication. "Find me," Elvis had said. "Look for my pride and joy and you will find me," he had said. But it didn't seem that I would find his pride and joy on the street outside.

Curtis had wandered a few yards away and studied the writing on the brown fieldstones of the fence. I caught up with him, and we edged our way down the sidewalk along the fence. It was covered with thousands of sayings in different-colored ink and marker and chalk. People stood in front of it; some leaned over, some knelt, one stretched up on his tiptoes. All of them were reading the words written there or writing messages to Elvis.

Curtis's eyes darted from one message to the next. He went to one knee and ran his finger over the surface of the stones as he read the many sayings tattooed on them.

I walked up behind him. "When was your dad here?" I asked.

"1971. Dad said what he wrote was on the right side of the gate and a few feet away from the brick."

I knelt beside him and began reading the countless messages along with him: "I Love You, Elvis." "We miss you, King." "Rock on Dude." The things written on the fence faded backward in time. Graffiti lay over graffiti. We searched stone by stone. The writing had built up through the years. The old had faded or had been partially washed off, the new written over it. It appeared as if the words were being absorbed into the stone. Names, places, and dates stretched down the fence—Charlotte, Mad Dog, Ronnie, Jack, Chung. People from all over the world—Canada, Bangkok, Brussels, Detroit, Tokyo, Alaska. All had something to say to him. "Elvis, I know you're all right in Heaven." "Elvis, you were in my dream and you were eating a fried peanut butter and banana sandwich." "Was that you I saw at Burger King?" "I am Elvis's love child." "In the name of Elvis, I eat cheese." "If I can dream, Elvis lives forever."

We went farther and farther down the fence. The oldest date I found was '6/07/1974.' I was barely able to make it out against a brown, flat stone. But we couldn't find the message Curtis was searching for. Those words were gone.

After an hour, I stopped and sat down at the edge of the sidewalk. A light drizzle started and increased to a steady rain. It was a relief from the penetrating heat and chased off the gnats. The rain pelted my head and body. Curtis kept searching. The expression on his face was intense. He stared at the fence like he was trying to pull the words he was searching for out from the stones. I didn't say anything to him. I wasn't sure he would even hear me if I did.

I stared through the gate, trying to figure out what I should do, trying to determine how I could possibly find Elvis, find his pride and joy. Nothing felt right. There were too many people around. And what I was looking for wouldn't be written on the fence; it wouldn't be outside on the street. What I was looking for would be something personal. Something private. Something that Elvis loved or used. Something that meant something to him. It would be on the grounds. Maybe in the house. Maybe near his grave. I needed to get in. But how? I buried my chin in my hands. It was hopeless.

Curtis walked over to me. "It's not here. It was all a bunch of bullshit." He tossed a small pebble to the sidewalk. "Like everything I ever got from him."

"It's probably been cleaned off over the years. I'm sure he really did it. You just have to believe it."

"Nah, it never happened." Curtis sat down and crossed his legs. He looked at the ground. "Let's get the hell out of here." His head was bowed, and his wet hair hung in tangles in front of his face. Large drops of water fell from the ends.

"No, I don't want to leave yet."

"What else are we going to do? There's nothing for us here. Come on." Curtis stood and took a step in the direction of our car.

I looked at the closed gate. Our whole trip couldn't end like this, to come all this way for nothing. I didn't want to give up, but I didn't know what I could do. I couldn't shake the feeling that it didn't seem right. I sat there while Curtis stared at me waiting for me to get up. I didn't have a choice. I couldn't bust through the gate and check out the grounds. I could sit there all day in the rain and still be no closer to finding what I was meant to find, still be sitting outside in the rain looking in.

"Come on, Jack. Let's get out of here."

I grunted, got up, and followed Curtis. With all that had happened and all that I had been through, I was mad. All of it was for nothing. My body was tense. My hands were balled into fists. I wanted to walk up to that stone fence and punch a hole right through it.

We went back to the car and drove away. The rain had increased, and drops pelted my arm as I sat in the passenger seat. I stared ahead at the road, searching my mind for what I was missing, for what else I could do.

Our wipers screeched back and forth across the windshield. I had my knees up on the dash and my back was curled against my seat. I held the Elvis statue in my hand and stared at it. I wanted it to talk. I wanted it to tell me what I should be looking for. I felt everything was slipping away from me. I had wanted so badly to find something of meaning there, to find Elvis. Whatever the hell that meant. Maybe it was all a bunch of bullshit like everything else.

"So I guess we head north now," Curtis said. His eyes were empty, like the life had been drained from him. His wet jeans squeaked against his plastic seat.

"North?" I put my feet on the floor and slid upright in the seat. "I don't know, Curtis. It's been tough out here. And I spent my last ten bucks the last time we filled up."

"What? We each left Carl's with about a hundred."

I paused. "I stuck sixty dollars into Becky's backpack."

He turned to me. "I don't believe you. What? Did she make you pay her for last night?"

"Shut up. It wasn't like that."

"How the hell are we going to make it anywhere without cash?" Curtis glanced to the side of the road and shook his head. "I knew we never should've let that girl come with us."

"It was my damn money." I thumped the Elvis statue onto the dash. "She saved our butts. If she hadn't distracted those cops, we'd be riding back to Tampa in cuffs right now."

"Man, you sabotaged us."

We drove on in silence. I sat there looking at that statue. I heard Elvis's voice, the one from my dreams. "Go back to Graceland, Jack. I'll be there for you. Trust me." The voice was clear and full and seemed to swell up through me. My heart raced. My eyes grew as I stared at the statue. I almost expected it to wink at me. I needed to go back. I needed to try to find whatever it was Elvis was talking about. I had to be sure. I couldn't give up. It would be dark in a few hours. We could hop the fence. I felt that Elvis was calling to me from his grave and that was where I had to go. The entrance ramp for the interstate was after the next light. Once we got on the interstate, there would be no turning back.

"Turn around." I leaned forward, rested my arm on the dash, and faced Curtis.

Curtis just looked at me.

"Pull off."

"Why?"

"Just do it. Pull over."

Curtis turned into a parking lot and stopped.

"I want to go back to Graceland."

"What? That's nuts."

"Come on. Let's go back. We can sneak in tonight, after it's dark."

He scrunched his face like he couldn't believe what I was saying. "We'll get busted."

"Once we hop the fence, we'll have the place to ourselves."

"Why do you want to go back?"

I ignored his question. "We could go all over the place. We could go into the Meditation Gardens and look at his gravestone. Wouldn't that be cool? We'd be the only ones there. Just us and Elvis."

"Yeah, just us and the security guards. No."

"We need to go back." I looked down at the seat. "Or I need to go back. You can let me out here."

Curtis and paused and studied me. He sighed. "Okay. We can go back. But what are you keeping from me?"

"What do you mean?"

"Come on. I can tell. There's more to it than you're letting on. Can you just tell me why you want to go back? Why is it so important to you?"

I looked at him. I owed him an explanation. Maybe that was the only way I could make him understand. But it would take a while to explain it all, and he would probably laugh at me when I got done. I let out a deep breath. "I'll tell you everything. Why don't we go somewhere. A restaurant or something. I'm hungry, and there's a lot I have to say. Besides, we have to wait till it's dark anyway."

We drove to a diner and took a booth at the window in front of

Curtis's Dart. We each had a burger and some fries. Curtis looked out the window and watched the cars go by while I told him everything. I told him about the dreams and how real they had seemed. I told him about how Elvis in the first dream warned me about the cop that was about to hassle us and in the second dream had told me how the golden arches would be our salvation. I told Curtis about how Elvis had told me to find him and to look for his pride and joy. And I told him about the voice I heard just a while ago telling me to go back. I even told him about how I had failed to save Elvis. Curtis sat there and took it all in. He nodded his head occasionally but never asked a question, never said one word.

When I was finished, I waited for him to crack up laughing at how crazy it all sounded. Curtis had his arms laid out across the table and sat low on the bench. I rested my face on my elbows. Beads of sweat ran down the soda glass in front of me.

He looked at me for a long moment. "Don't go blaming yourself for what happened with that Elvis guy. He made his choice."

The thought of that pained me. "Yeah, I know." But I didn't know. I looked down at the tabletop.

Curtis leaned forward and picked up the paper wrapper for his straw. He twisted it tight around his finger. "He was a shyster. He probably thought that lady would give him some kind of reward or something."

I shook my head. "When he was lying there all busted up and dying, the first thing he did was ask about that kid."

Curtis held the wrapper tight, pinching it between his thumb and middle finger. The tip of his finger bulged up. "My old man used to say that there isn't anyone in this world that's ever going to do anything for you but you. That was about the only thing I ever agreed with him on. Elvis was trying to be a hero. In the big wide world, what he did don't mean nothing."

I clenched my straw between my teeth. "That shit."

"That shit." The tip of Curtis's finger was beet red. He stared at it. "Sometimes, shit just happens. Like with that old man that day.

You think if I knew that stupid old man was going to get shot, I would've done what I did?"

We hadn't talked about that day since we set out on the road. A couple of times, Curtis had referred to that "stupid old man," and I knew who he was talking about. But we had referred to the event simply as "It." Somehow that allowed us to accept "It." It made "It" seem like "It" never really happened. Even though the last few weeks we had lived under the shadow of "It," like we were standing under the growing shadow of a boulder falling off a cliff toward us.

"Curtis, what do you think would've happened if we would've let that man take us in that day like he wanted?"

"It doesn't matter what would've happened. That's not what happened."

"Yeah, but just say we had."

"I don't know." He took a fork and lightly jabbed one of the tines against the tip of his finger.

"We wouldn't be on the run now. We would've already dealt with whatever trouble we were going to get into."

"You mean I'd be in jail. You might be in jail now too." He thought about it. "Maybe not. It wasn't really that bad until he got shot." He shook his head. "It doesn't matter."

"Yeah, you're right there, but there was something about that night before we got caught. That's when we really crossed the line."

"Yeah, we lost it that night. You can only keep things bottled up inside of you for so long."

I plunged my straw into my drink and sucked soda through it, but air came in through the small holes I had chewed into it. It made a funny bubbly sound. "That fire could've gotten out of control real easy in all those dry pine needles. We could've burned down that whole damn forest and not even given a crap about it. But the next day is when we had to pay for all that stuff we'd done."

"Yeah, that stupid old man. He couldn't let it go."

"I bet he wishes he had now." I pulled my straw from my drink and held it above the table. A few drops of Coke splashed in front of me. "Maybe we should turn ourselves in."

"What? No!"

"How long can we stay out on the run?"

"I'm not going back. Ever."

"Why not? It might not be as bad as you think. It was an accident."

"I don't think the law is going to see it like that." He pulled his wrapper tighter. The wrapper snapped and fell from around his finger. "That's the difference between Elvis and me. He does something in the heat of the moment, and he ends up dead, but he saves some stupid kid. I do something, and I end up shooting some guy in the gut, and now I have to live with it. Both of us paid for what we did with our lives, the only difference is I get to keep breathing." Curtis balled up the paper wrapper between his thumb and index finger and flicked it onto the table. He looked me hard in the eye. His brow furrowed. "I'm never going back."

We sat in that diner for hours sipping Cokes and talking. We waited until dark and beyond, until we reached the heart of the night. And that's when we made our way back to Graceland. That seemed fitting—it was the heart of the night when all this lunatic stuff really began for us anyway.

# Sacred Ground

After Curtis parked the Dart, I grabbed the Elvis statue off the dashboard and slipped it into my pocket, and we walked to Graceland through a light rain. The dull glow of the streetlights glared off the wet road and lit millions of water specks drifting directionless in the air. We stopped across the street and scoped things out. I don't know what we were looking for. Mostly, I think we were gathering our courage, looking for a good place to hop the fence and waiting for a break in the constant passing of cars.

When there was a pause in traffic, Curtis grabbed my arm and hauled me along with him. "Come on." We marched to the far corner of the fence, as far away from the guard shack as possible.

I clasped my hands together and leaned over in front of him. "I'll give you a boost."

Curtis put his foot into my hands, stepped up, and grabbed the top. He hefted himself up and poked his head over, supporting himself with his arms.

"Do you see any guards?" I asked.

Curtis twisted his head one way, then the other. "No, I don't see anyone." Curtis swung his leg up and set his foot on the top. He lifted himself up and over. "Come on," he called back.

I grabbed the top of the fence and dragged myself up. My feet slipped several times off the wet stones, but I managed to lift myself enough so I could plant my shoe on top of the jagged fence and push myself over. I dropped down next to Curtis.

We knelt at the base of the fence, hiding in the shadow there. Up the sloping yard, two lights glowed above the front door of Graceland, but the inside was dark. It seemed empty. Light from the guard shack behind the large brick column of the gate made an oval on the wet asphalt of the driveway. The light was broken by the shadow of a man who walked in front of the window.

We ran up toward the house and hopped the white rail fence that separated the paddock from the yard. We kept low, trying to keep from the view of the guard shack. We stopped at a hedge beneath a window covered with wrought-iron bars. The leaves glistened with moisture and blinked when raindrops glanced off them. I tried to peer into the house, but the drapes were closed.

We rounded the side of the house and saw a circular brick structure next to a swimming pool. "That's the Meditation Gardens." I grabbed Curtis by the arm. "That's where he's buried." I led him to it.

At the entrance to the enclosure, several lamps dimly lit the stained glass windows set in the brick wall that surrounded the garden. A shallow pool sat in the center. Submerged lights illuminated several small fountains that clapped the surface. A statue of Jesus with one hand raised stood at the edge. I entered the structure slowly.

We walked down the stairs and around the perimeter of the short fence that surrounded the pool and stopped at the foot of his grave.

I shuffled back a step and took it all in. The eternal flame, encased in glass, wavered at the head of Elvis's gravestone. Three small statues of angels sat below, their heads bent to the side looking down at it. Flowers lined the edge of the slab, slumped over from the rain that splattered the stone and pooled on the bronze plaque covering his grave. The shallow puddles twitched as drops hit them.

Curtis stood with his hands on the railing of the short fence. He gazed at the grave with a thousand-yard stare. "So that's how it ends, huh." He spoke softly, as if he didn't want to violate the sanctity of the air around us. "You end up six feet under with the cold rain pelting your stone."

"Yeah, even someone like Elvis." A chill ran through me. I folded my arms across my chest. "I feel him here. Like he's looking down at me from somewhere. Like he can see into my heart, see the kind of person I am." I shook my head. "I guess that sounds stupid."

Curtis kept his eyes locked on Elvis's grave. "No, that's not stupid. I feel my father watching me sometimes. I wish it were Elvis. You know, if my dad ever saw me sitting in his chair, he would look at me like he wanted to kill me or something and tell me to get up. It didn't matter if he was planning to sit in it or not." His hands tightened on the railing; his shoulders pushed up. "After he died, I sat in that chair for hours and smoked one of his cigars. I felt him watching me, judging me from wherever the hell he was. And wherever the hell he was, I knew he was pissed at me for sitting in his goddamn chair. That's when I took the cigar and put it out on the arm." He took a deep breath. He twisted to look at me and smiled. His teeth glowed white from the darkness. "And as I did it, I felt totally satisfied. Like I was showing him. Showing him he didn't have anything on me anymore. Showing him I was free of him, but part of me knew I wasn't free of him. Not at all."

"He was hard on you, Curtis," I said. "That kind of shit sticks with you."

"Yeah," he turned away.

We stood there looking at Elvis's grave, listening to the fountains slap the surface of the pool. The air smelled clean; the rain fell steadily. My jeans and shirt were soaked. They felt cold against my skin.

Curtis broke away from the short rail fence and took a step toward me. "So, what are we looking for?" he asked.

"He told me to look for his pride and joy."

"Pride and joy, huh? That's probably not his grave."

"Yeah." I shrugged. I had no idea what to look for, really.

"He loved his cars. Maybe he was talking about them."

I straightened. "That must be it." I grabbed Curtis by the arm and pulled him after me.

We left the gardens and went past the pool. A long carport connected the house and a small white building with a short fence in front. It looked like a small office. We ran to it. The dark shapes of three cars sat on the floor of the carport. I probed the wall for a light switch. I found it and flipped it.

"Shut it off," Curtis said. "The guard is going to catch us for sure."

"We'll just keep it on for a minute."

Underneath the light, in the middle of the carport, was Elvis's 1973 Stutz Blackhawk. A lot of people associate a pink Cadillac with Elvis. But he owned that car in the late 50's. The truth was, the Blackhawk was the car he drove at the end of his life. In fact, he drove it just twelve hours before he died. I remembered reading that he had to go to the dentist.

I walked slowly around the Blackhawk that gleamed in the pale light of the carport. The headlights were chrome dots that seemed too small for the grill. Its bright spoke wheels nested within whitewall tires.

I went to the driver's side door and tried the handle. I was surprised when the door latch released. I pulled it open and eased my way in. A strip of wood grain panel on the driver and passenger doors cut a swathe through the bright red leather. All details of the interior were gold-plated. As I slid across the seat, my wet pants burped.

Curtis turned the light off, then got into the car.

I left my door open so the inside light stayed on and put my hands on the red steering wheel with three silver prongs embedded in the center, like a 'T.' It felt cold and slick. I rolled down the window and rested my arm on the door, keeping one hand on the wheel.

This had to be what Elvis was talking about. This must be his pride and joy. As I sat there, holding onto the steering wheel, I felt like I had done exactly what he wanted me to do. I had made it to the place that I was meant to find. I was close to what he had promised, close to finding him. I knew it. I pulled the statue out of my pocket and set it on the dash.

"Come on," I said. "There has to be something here for me."

"What?"

"I have no idea." I tried to open the glove compartment, but it was locked. I felt the floor under the seat. Curtis searched underneath his seat too. But we couldn't find so much as a bottle cap on the floor. There was nothing there. Nothing at all. I leaned over into the back seat and felt around on the floor and shoved my hand into the gap between the back and bottom of the seat. Still nothing. I glared at the statue in front of me, wanting it to tell me what I needed to do, tell me what I was meant to find here.

I heard Elvis's voice: "You did it, Jack."

Did what? I didn't do anything. That couldn't be it. I clenched my teeth and tightened my grasp on the steering wheel, twisting my hands like I was trying to snap it in half. There had to be more. I wanted to find something. Something I could take with me. Something I could hold as proof of the dreams, of all that happened. Something that was significant. Something that meant something. After all I had been through, I deserved it. But I realized I wasn't going to get it. I slumped back into the driver's seat. I sat there wringing the steering wheel with my hands, trying to keep my anger in check.

"Let's get out of here," Curtis said.

"And go where? Canada?"

"Yeah."

"No. It's time we went back."

Curtis looked down and said nothing.

"It's time we stopped running. Both of us."

Curtis pressed his lips tight together and shook his head. "You should go back. You'd be better off."

"You should come back too."

"Not a chance."

"Why? Shooting that old man was an accident. He was the one that pulled the gun on us. It wasn't even our gun."

"You don't understand."

"I don't understand what?"

He was silent; his head was bent, his gaze to the floor. "Do you think the gun just went off?"

I didn't say anything.

"Do you?" He turned to look at me. "Well, it didn't." Anger swelled in his voice. "I clicked off the safety. I shoved the gun into that old man's gut, and I pulled the trigger. I shot that old man on purpose. I shot that old man because I was pissed, and I wanted to hurt him. Don't you get it?"

My eyes grew wide. My jaw dropped open. A hole opened up in my heart. I shook my head back and forth, struggling to believe what he was telling me. "Nobody knows that."

"Any cop is going to know it. Any lawyer or judge is going to know it. Even Bruce knew it. The only one who didn't know it was you. That look on your face says it all."

"Curtis, it was a mistake. That's all. You got caught up in the moment."

"No! No, I didn't! That's not it. I ain't no good, man. Don't you see that?"

I looked out the window, searching the darkness in the yard outside the carport, searching for something I knew I wouldn't find out there. I turned back toward Curtis. "You have to live with it, Curtis. You have to move on. You can't change what's happened."

"You can't get away from it either. And what's happened can sure twist you up inside." Curtis looked down, dropping his chin almost to his chest.

I stretched my hand out toward him to touch him, to give him any assurance that I could, but I pulled it back before it reached him.

Curtis took a deep breath and shook his head. "It was like that day, in my father's chair. That's exactly how I felt when that gun exploded into that old man's gut, like I was showing him. For a minute. But then . . ." He put his hand to his face. His body shuddered. "That's what goes through my head. Sometimes I can't stand myself."

I looked at Curtis, my best friend, and tried to think of anything that I could say to him, anything that would help him, that would make him feel better about himself and what happened, that would give him some hope that he could move past it, that he could find something in this world to cling to. Some magic words that would somehow chase those demons from his head. But there was nothing I could say. There was nothing I could do for him.

He fell back against the seat and arched his back. "I don't know what makes me like that." He thumped his head against the headrest. Tears ran down his face. "You know I felt cheated when he died. The last couple of days, he was completely out of it. You didn't know whether he knew you were there or not. I hated seeing him like that. He was so weak."

"He was dying."

"Yeah, But I still…in the end…I wanted something from him." He folded his arms across his chest like he was holding himself. "I don't know what I expected. Recognition. Approval. I guess that's stupid. He never had a good word for me his whole life. Why would he save it for when he was dying? But the thing that really pissed me off was that I never got a chance to say anything to him…to tell him . . ."

"Tell him what?"

Curtis started to say something but stopped himself. Pain racked his face. "That I—" He just couldn't say it. But he didn't need to. I understood. I understood how he felt when his father died, how he felt when he was sitting in that hospital room with him, watching him waste away. Even after everything his father had done to him, even though his father treated him like crap his whole life. Curtis still loved him and wished he had been able to tell him that before he died.

"It's all right, Curtis."

He nodded and bit his lip. "I was so pissed at him the day he died."

"Is that why you—" I stopped myself.

He turned toward me. He knew I was talking about his suicide attempt. Curtis squinted his eyes. "Yeah. But you know, in the ambulance. That night. After I did it," he said. "You'd think that I would've been freaking out and shaking and everything, but I lay there in the ambulance and felt at peace, like I was free of it all. Finally."

"Would you try it again?"

"I don't know." He wiped his eyes. "I'm hopeless." There was a long silence. "Nah, I wouldn't try that again."

Curtis got out of the car. He stood at the open door and leaned in toward me. He took a final deep breath and blew it out. "You've been my only friend. You're the only one who ever saw any good in me," he said. "I'm leaving you and you need to let me go." Curtis walked away.

I put both my hands on the steering wheel and leaned against it. I looked at the small statue of Elvis on the dashboard in front of me. Tears started to well in my eyes. A part of me wanted to get up and follow Curtis, to stay with him no matter what, but I knew he was right. I wasn't going any farther.

"What are you doing?"

I looked in the rearview mirror. Curtis's leaned against the trunk of the car. Someone stood in front of him, but I couldn't see them.

"Nothing," Curtis said

"How did you get in here?"

"I must've got lost." Curtis stepped to the side and reached into his pocket.

"Don't move!"

"Just let me go!" Curtis took out his knife and opened the blade. He held the knife out in front of himself.

"Put that down!"

I rolled to the side and eased my way out the door. I dropped to the ground on my hands and knees. I crawled to the back of the car and glanced around the corner. The security guard was a young man. Maybe in his twenties. His legs were spread, and he was leaning back.

He held his gun with both hands, pointing it at Curtis. The barrel was shaking. "Stay back!" He took a step backwards.

I poked my head out farther.

Curtis moved forward, the knife in his hand. "Step out of my way."

I crouched at the end of the car. My heart pounded. Neither of them noticed me. They were intent on each other. Curtis took another step forward. His chest was puffed out. His mouth was in a sneer. His eyes were narrow and focused on that guard. His hands were held low, balled into fists, one clutching the knife. He took another step. He was huge compared to the guard. He looked like a rhino set to charge Bambi. I knew by looking at him that was his plan. The guard would have to put a bullet into Curtis's chest to stop him. And one way or another, Curtis would get what he wanted. One way or another, Curtis wasn't going to be arrested and thrown in jail.

"Don't make me!" the guard said.

I was three short steps away from them. My body tensed, as I tried to decide what to do. If I went after Curtis and tackled him, I might be able to hold him and maybe take the knife from his hand. I could help the guard arrest him. Curtis wouldn't hurt me. I was sure of that. But if I went after the guard, I could help Curtis get away. Help Curtis get back on the run. I could give him what he wanted, give him his freedom for a while longer. I wasn't sure what I should do. The only thing I knew for sure was that this time I wasn't going to freeze. This time at least I would do something.

Curtis took another step. The guard steadied his hand, ready to fire.

I drove my body forward and lunged at the guard. He saw me and started to turn, swinging the gun toward me. I dove, plowing into him, burying my head in the center of his gut and pulling both his arms down. He stumbled backward and fell. I crashed down on top of him. The gun went off. A blast of hot air hit my gut. I felt pain. I thought I had landed on the gun. I clung to the guard, pinning him to the ground. "Run, Curtis!"

"Let me go!" the guard said. He jammed the palm of his hand into the side of my face, trying to shove me away. But I held on. I turned my head back to Curtis. He stood there looking at me.

"Just go!"

The guard pried his hands free of me and started to wiggle himself out of my grasp. Curtis turned. He ran out of the light and disappeared into the darkness. He was gone. I continued to hold the guard to give Curtis time. The guard pulled free and climbed to his feet.

"You aren't getting away," he said. He hovered over me with the gun in his hand.

I rolled to my back. Pain shot through me.

The guard's eyes bulged, looking at me. "Shit! You've been shot."

I looked down at my gut. A circle of blood spread across the side of my T-shirt from a hole that was shiny and burping blood. I pressed my hand over the wound. Warm blood coursed over my fingers. I lifted my hand and looked at it draining down like strawberry syrup. My mind started to swim. A ringing grew in my head. My hand flopped to the floor. My knuckles knocked onto the concrete. Everything dimmed; the room drifted away from me.

# Elvis Sings

I lie on the ground, blood oozing from my side. Elvis stands above me. He is young. Cleancut and shining. Like brand-new. He smiles; the right side of his lip peaks slightly. He doesn't say a word, but his gaze holds me captivated.

He turns, walks away, then looks back and waves for me to follow. I point at my wound, at the blood spilling on the ground around me. He puffs out a chuckle. He waves his hand, and the wound shrinks away to nothing. I climb to my feet. He nods and continues on.

He leads me to a doorway. The door is halfway open, and light spills out in a bright shaft. Lively chatter bubbles from the opening and surrounds us. He pulls the door fully open and ushers me through.

The room is filled with hundreds of Elvises. There are Elvises from all the periods of his life. Young Elvises. Old Elvises. Elvises from each of his movies. Elvises from when he was in the army. Vegas Elvises. Black-and-white television Elvises. The one from the *Ed Sullivan Show* raises his drink to me and nods. Every image of Elvis I have ever seen is there. They're holding drinks and talking with each other. Laughing and slapping each other on the back. All of them are having a great time sharing each other's company.

I walk out among them, wondering at them. At first they don't notice me—then they all turn and smile. They gather around me, gravitating toward me. The chatter becomes louder. More and more of them pull in close to me. They start pressing in on me, squeezing me. My arms are pinned. They begin crushing me. I cry out for them to stop, but they continue to press closer. I can't move. I gasp and struggle to draw in breath. Light swells up from below us, becoming brighter and brighter. It radiates through the air and bursts forth from all the Elvises. They vanish in a flash.

Everything goes black. And silent. And empty.

I am alone.

Cold penetrates me. It creeps into my core.

I hold myself, trying to keep in any remaining warmth. My breath comes from me in icy puffs.

The sound of a piano rolls through the air from the distance.

I recognize the tune: "Unchained Melody." I move toward it. I am shuddering. A voice emerges. It's too far away to hear it clearly, but it's Elvis. Singing beautifully. Perfectly. I go toward the music. His voice is strong and wonderful, exactly like the recording that I loved so much. I feel warmth growing within me. The cold melts away from me.

". . . I hunger for your touch . . ."

A spotlight focuses on a grand piano. Elvis is seated at it. Wearing one of his jumpsuits. The music grows louder. It radiates through me. It fills me. It draws me toward it.

". . . I need your love. I need your love . . ."

I approach the piano, slowly, cautiously, not wanting to spoil his performance. I place my hand gently on the polished black wood. He continues playing and singing. It is the Elvis from near the end of his life. He is overweight. His skin is pale and doughy. His cheeks are pocked. He finishes playing and turns toward me. His jaw gapes slightly, and his jowls droop like a Bassett hound's. "Well, you made it, Jack." His breathing is labored and heavy and, at times, shakes the microphone. His eyes are dull and weary.

"I failed."

"No, you didn't." Elvis nods to the top of the piano. The Elvis statue rests there in front of him. "You saved it."

"That's what I was supposed to save? But a man lost his life. I could've saved him."

"Maybe. Maybe not." Elvis studies me. "Some things are meant to happen. Some things are meant to be. You did your best. That's all you can do. That's all anyone can do. Don't be so hard on yourself."

"But what does it all mean?"

"Mean?" He leans into the microphone and exhales. His breath rattles over the speaker. "It doesn't have to mean anything."

"But it does. You're Elvis. You're the King."

"Jack, there was nothing special about me. People loved me for what I did, not for who I was. I had a gift. I could sing. And I used that gift to touch people, to make them feel better about themselves. Better about their lives. That was a blessing that God granted me. But I was just a man. No better or worse than anyone. I wanted the same things that you want." He shrugs. "The same things everyone wants. I had the same hopes. The same fears."

"Fears? What are you afraid of?"

His eyes widen. He recoils. "Being abandoned." His face sags. "Being forgotten." He looks down. "Being alone." He shakes his head. "Nobody wants to be alone, Jack. Not in the end. Everyone is looking for someone or something then. Something they can cling to. That's all any of us can hope for, really."

"Am I dead?"

He lifts his gaze to me. "No, Jack. You're not dead." He smiles. "You're going home." He leans forward; his hands hover over the piano. "But before you go—" His eyes search me, implore me. He begins to play, his fingers rolling over the keys. "Could you do one thing for me?"

"What, Elvis? What do you need?"

"Could you…could you listen to me one more time? Just one more time. Listen to that song you loved so much. Let me sing it for you. One last time. Please."

He begins to sing.

# *Breathing Underwater*

I woke up in a Memphis hospital. My side felt like someone had shoved a red hot spike into it, and every few minutes, when it started to cool, replaced it with a fresh redhot spike. Mom was sitting in a chair by my bed. She had made the trip north. When she saw my eyes open, she told the nurse and the nurse told the doctor. They all came in and surrounded me. The doctor asked me how I felt. I told him about the spike. He said he could give me something for the pain and that the bullet passed down the front of my abdomen, making a trough. The bullet didn't go through me or anything, but it took out a chunk of my colon. The doctor said he was able to sew it up: good as new. They told me that I almost died from blood loss. He said that I was lucky, but I didn't feel very lucky.

They showed me a newspaper article about me being shot. The security guard at Graceland saved my life. He applied pressure to my wound to slow the bleeding until the paramedics could get there. The papers made him out like a hero, even though he was the guy that shot me in the first place. I guess so. I mean, he did save my life.

After the nurse and the doctor left, Mom lost it. She went back and forth between crying and yelling at me. If I wasn't already in a lot of pain, she would've yelled at me more. All I could do was tell her that I was sorry. And I was.

The powers that be at Graceland decided not to press charges, mostly because I got shot and almost died. They figured that was enough punishment. And they got some good press about the security guard saving me. The state of Florida was not quite so agreeable, so Mom got a lawyer for me.

That next week, when I was released from the hospital, Mom drove me back to face my charges in Florida.

I never spent any time in jail in Tampa. My lawyer arranged for bail, and I met with the judge, entered my plea, and got a court date. My lawyer said that I was lucky because technically I was still a minor while Curtis was an adult, but I might have to do some time. That was in the future, something I had to look forward to. For the moment anyway, I was free. As free as was possible for me, I guess.

It was weird going back home. I knew it would be. My grandfather always said that you could never go back, and he was right. Home was never the same again. But at least it was still there. Still with me, in some ways. In the past. In my heart. And it always would be, even though I couldn't quite touch it any more.

Curtis stayed on the run and no one heard anything from him. But I didn't hang out or talk much to anyone when I got back. I didn't talk to Bruce at all. I didn't avoid him. But I sure as hell wasn't going to track him down.

A week after I got back to Tampa, I saw a headline on the cover of the *National Enquirer,* in bold print, next to a picture of Elizabeth Taylor eating a chicken wing: "Elvis Killed on Highway Fifty Miles South of Memphis after Saving Life of Youth."

It was a big article in the dead center of the magazine with several pictures. Some looked like they were taken from a helicopter. There was one of Elvis lying on the grass where I left him with my T-shirt covering his face. Another of Becky in the arms of one of the cops with the caption: "Elvis's love interest consoled by law enforce-ment officer." Another picture showed that woman and her two kids standing there with dumb expressions on their faces. The article was a bunch of crap, mostly, except for talking about how Elvis saved that kid.

It went on to say that Elvis had spent the last five years selling Bibles and religious trinkets door to door in a sky-blue pickup truck. Becky was mentioned prominently in the article as Elvis's young fe-male assistant. There was a sidebar interview with her—not sure if they made that up too, but it sure sounded like her. She said she had been riding with him from town to town, and, now that he was gone, she was going on to fulfill the vision he had for her: to be a Hollywood movie star.

I kept waiting to hear from Curtis. I expected him to show up one day after being hauled back in chains or to come back on his own. But the weeks counted up without any word from him or about him. I was feeling pretty restless about it.

As I waited to see what would happen with my court case, my life was in limbo. My lawyer recommended I find a job. He told me that they might go easier on me. Of course, it was a month before I was healthy enough to work after my wound. But it didn't take me long to find something.

It was at a concrete company, mixing concrete for big cement mixers. It was pretty crappy work. I probably inhaled enough dust in one day to cough out a cinder block. I went in at three in the morn-ing and worked till noon. The pay wasn't bad.

After I brought home a couple paychecks, I had enough money to get my own apartment. I had turned eighteen, and it was time I got out on my own. But beyond that, I didn't know what the hell I wanted to do. I still had my impending court case hanging over me. That put a question mark after any long-term plans I wanted to make. The apartment was a dumpy place right on the corner of a busy intersection in Tampa, but that was all I could afford.

•••••••••••

A couple weeks after I moved into my apartment, I got a letter from Becky. The postmark was from Los Angeles.

Dear Jack,

I hope you get this. I know you weren't too sure whether you would head back home or not. Somehow, I had the feeling you would, especially since you gave me your home address. I hope everything worked out all right for you and Curtis.

I made it to California. My cousin set me up with a job. And it's in the movies! I'm selling popcorn and Raisinets at a six-theatre complex there. Not as glamorous as I thought. Well, I guess that's show biz. At least I get to watch all the movies for free. I sneak home popcorn and hot dogs. I've got a crappy little efficiency close enough to walk to work. I pay my rent by the week, and it's cheap, but that's about the best thing I can say about it. Other than that, I really like it out here. The beach is close by. I like going there when I'm not working.

I'm starting to get the urge to move on again. I don't know where, though. Sometimes, I think about that night we were together tucked in my sleeping bag and that makes me smile. I hope you think about me sometimes too. Maybe one of these days, I'll head your way. ☺

Love, Becky

It was nice to hear from her. I read her letter a couple of times, and then I sat down and wrote back. I told her about all the stuff that happened, about me getting arrested and shot and everything, and how I would love to see her and thought about her a lot too.

•••••••••••

Two nights later, Curtis's mom called. I knew the minute I heard her voice something was wrong. She told me they found his body in his car in a river near Chicago.

The story she gave me was that Curtis was living on the street, trying to get money any way he could and sleeping in his car. They told her that he fell asleep behind the wheel and drove off a bridge. She said it was an accident. Someone witnessed his car hitting the water, but it sank before anyone could save him.

After I heard that, I pictured Curtis clutching onto the steering wheel at the bottom of the river, his teeth gritted, his face twisted and blue, frozen like time stopped and wouldn't let him go on. I shuddered when I thought of it. That image still haunts me sometimes.

"Did you know he was going to Chicago?" Her voice broke. She started crying.

"No," I said. "I had no idea."

"Okay." She paused and gathered herself. "You were his friend." She said it like she was accusing me, then burst into tears.

I told her I was sorry. I told her it was all right. I told her he was my best friend. She started talking again, but I didn't hear anything she said. I felt guilty as hell the whole time. When she finished, I asked her if there was anything I could do. She said, "No."

After she hung up, I felt like someone had cut open my chest and emptied out everything inside. I sat in my room and thought about everything: about Curtis, about myself, about that last night I saw him at Graceland, about what would've happened if I had tackled him instead of that security guard.

I wished like hell for somebody to talk to. But I didn't have any real friends around, you know, someone that I could call up and spill out my guts to. Everyone needs someone like that. Curtis was like that for me, and I sure needed someone that night, because I felt shitty as hell.

It was cold and raining and pitch dark. I know it was nighttime, but a lot of times, you'll see shadows of things. You can kind of make stuff out. I looked out the window through my reflection, and there was nothing out there, not even a streetlight. It was like staring into a pan of used motor oil.

I couldn't stand it. I went for a walk. I didn't care that it was raining. I didn't care that it was cold. Mostly, I just didn't care. I got drenched. You should've seen some of the looks I got. The other people out thought I was a freak. Everybody else was hiding under an umbrella or had some kind of plastic coat on.

I didn't feel the cold for the longest time; I guess because I was so upset. When I did notice it, I was freezing. I must've looked like a drowned rat too. My arms were folded across my chest, and I held myself. My hair hung down into my eyes. I kept blowing water off my upper lip. I started shivering.

Some bald-headed guy walked past me holding a section of newspaper over himself. That made me laugh. He probably gave me the dirtiest look of all. I asked him, "Nice night, isn't it?" He had to smile. I must've looked like a nut. Shivering and shaking like I was without even a coat or anything. I went back to my apartment.

Later that night, I lay awake and listened to the slow hum of cars as they approached and passed, hissing over the thin layer of water on the street. I felt drawn to the sound. I thought how peaceful it would be out there, on the road, driving through the night, hearing nothing but the roar of the engine and the tires grinding the asphalt. Everything reduced to merely following my own headlights, nothing beyond that. I thought about getting up and driving out into the night, driving away and never coming back.

· · · · · · · · · · ·

Curtis's funeral was in a small church beside the Hillsborough River. It was a warm day, but windy. His mom stood next to the casket when I entered. A picture of Curtis sat on top of it. It was his high school picture. He hated that picture. He said it made him look too serious. He was right.

I sat down and waited for the service to begin. Whenever the front door of the church opened, wind surged in. I turned toward the door every time to see who was entering. Several people from school came. I was surprised at how many.

Bruce walked in and sat a couple rows behind me. We nodded to each other. With each person that came in, the wind got stronger and stronger. It knocked over a couple of the floral arrangements that stood by the casket. The funeral director immediately went over and set them right. One time, it knocked over Curtis's picture. That made me smile. Curtis would've liked that.

The pastor talked about Curtis and how young he was and what a shame it was. He told a story about some Christmas present Curtis gave his mom five years ago. I could tell the pastor didn't know anything about Curtis. The story didn't have anything to do with the Curtis I went to Graceland with. It didn't have anything to do with the Curtis that died in his car in Chicago. Sitting there listening to that guy talk made me mad. I don't know, maybe I was looking for this guy to draw some conclusion for me about Curtis, to tie his life up in some nice understandable bundle that I could file away. But that didn't happen. All he knew was what Curtis's mom had told him he was like, and she didn't have a clue.

After the service, I followed Bruce out. He had his hands in his pockets, and his shoulders were slumped.

"So have you settled your court case from the shooting?" I called ahead to him.

He turned. "Yeah, I got community service and a year's probation. What about you?"

"I have a court date next Friday. My lawyer said that I might have to do a little time. But maybe not. Getting shot may have helped me a little."

Bruce nodded. "Good plan." He turned away and shuffled across the parking lot. "That whole weekend was stupid. What was the point of it?" He stopped at his car, reached into his pocket, and pulled out his keys. "You could've come back with me. You would've gotten off easier."

"He was my friend. You can't always do the thing that's best for yourself." I jabbed my hands down into my pockets as I stopped in front of him.

"He was my friend, too." Bruce looked down. He was shaking. Maybe he felt guilty about leaving us that day. In a way, Bruce turned his back on Curtis. I didn't blame him. I felt like I had done the same thing. "What was he trying to prove?" Bruce asked.

"He wasn't trying to prove anything. He was trying to figure some things out."

"What?"

I thought about it for a minute then looked down at the ground. "I don't know."

"Why didn't he come back?"

"Maybe he didn't know how. Maybe he couldn't. Maybe he was just lost."

Bruce took a deep breath and reached for his car door. "You really think he was lost?" Bruce cocked his head to the side as he stuck his key in the door.

"Maybe."

Bruce nodded slightly and got into his car. I watched him back up and drive away.

• • • • • • • • • • •

Two days later, when I came home from work, Becky was sitting in the hallway of my apartment complex, backpack beside her, reading a book. I dropped the bags of groceries I was carrying, ran to her, and hugged her. I buried my nose into her neck and started to cry. So much had happened since I had seen her, and I was so glad that she had come to see me.

"Careful," she said. "You're going to break my spine." But she was smiling.

I let her into my apartment and asked her what she was doing here. She told me that she got sick of California and was thinking about me. I asked her how long she was going to stay. She said she wasn't sure. I told her she was welcome to stay as long as she wanted.

I took her to a Cuban restaurant near where I lived. After we finished eating, we stayed and drank coffee and talked. I asked Becky where she was heading after Florida. She told me she wanted to move up north.

"Why do you want to go north?" I tore open a packet of sugar as I started on my third cup. Some of the sugar spilled across the table.

"I want to live in a lighthouse." Becky gazed at the small mess I had made.

I almost busted a gut laughing. "A lighthouse?"

She had to laugh too. She told me that ever since she was a little girl she'd wanted to live in one, so she could save ships at night.

"I'd love to go up north too." I stirred my coffee. "And get away from this place."

"Do you want to go up north, or do you want to just get away from where you are?"

"A little of both." I tapped the coffee spoon on the side of my cup and set it on the table.

She laughed and picked up the spoon. I sipped my coffee.

"Do you think he committed suicide?" she asked.

"He had tried before. He might have."

"Why?"

"I don't know. He was looking for something he didn't find. I guess that's what we were both doing really; trying to find something."

"Did you find it?" She moved the grains of sugar around on the tabletop as if she were trying to organize them.

I shook my head and took a sip from my steaming cup of coffee. "I don't think so." I set the cup back on the table.

"What about Curtis?" She opened a packet of sugar and poured it on the table in a small pile. She spread the sugar evenly with the spoon.

"I think even if he'd found what he was looking for, it wouldn't have been enough for him. With Curtis, his dad was always at the core. His dad didn't give a crap about Curtis, but somehow Curtis still loved him."

"Sometimes, we love the people in our lives unconditionally. It doesn't matter how they treat us or whether they deserve it."

"Yeah, and sometimes we give the people we love what they want instead of what they need." I looked at her, then back down at the table. "What if I hadn't tackled that security guard? What if I had tackled Curtis instead? He probably would've been arrested with me. He might be alive now."

"You don't know that." She had dispersed the sugar as evenly as she could in a small patch on the table. It was spread thinly, almost like the stars in the sky.

"I know things would've turned out differently."

"You just wanted to help your friend. You couldn't have known how things were going to turn out."

"I should've known." I nodded my head. "I knew Curtis better than anyone."

"What did you really know about him?"

I paused and thought about her question. All I knew about Curtis, the only thing that I could say for sure, was that he was my friend and that he liked Elvis. Everything else, I would have to guess about. It made me sad to realize that, but at the same time, I knew it was true.

I asked her if she wanted to go down to the river. It was a clear night with a three-quarter moon. We went to a park near the university. We held hands as we walked to a pavilion near the bank. The river burbled lightly. Wrinkles spread across the water, black like crude oil.

We stood under the pavilion, and I kissed her warm, receptive lips, my mouth roaming over hers and then down her neck. I ended on my knees, my head resting against her stomach. She stretched her fingers through my hair. I pushed her back against the cement picnic table and undid her pants before I sat her on top of it. We writhed against each other. I felt her until she moaned softly under me, and I peeled off her remaining clothing. We ended with both of our bodies heaving. I told her that I loved her. She laughed—not mean, but like she didn't believe me, like I was caught up in the moment. I guess I was, really.

I got up from the table. The brighter white skin of the scar from my gunshot wound glowed in the moonlight. Becky placed her palm on my stomach to hold me and studied it. She touched it lightly with her finger, then kissed it. I stepped away from her, went down to the water, and then looked back. She moved around the table, gathering her clothes like tiny flowers.

I dove into the river. The water flowed around me and pushed me downstream. I swam against the current to the middle and plunged down until I reached the bottom. I clutched onto a handful of weeds and knelt on the soft mud-floor. Surrounded by all the blackness of water, I held myself against the current. It was so quiet there, so peaceful. My lungs ached to breathe. My knees sank into the mud. I wondered how Curtis felt in his last few moments, just before he took his first breath of the icy water. I tilted my head back and looked up. The moon rippled on the surface. I could even make out its scars and blemishes. I longed for it, to reach out for the image wavering above me, to touch it in some way.

I knelt on the bottom until I couldn't bear the pain in my chest. I pushed up and stretched out with my hand. The pain spurred me on. I kicked my feet, swimming toward the surface against the current, straining for the light wobbling above me. I burst through and emerged in the night air.

•••••••••••

Becky stayed with me for a week. I asked her to stay longer, but she wanted to get back out on the road. I guess she'll never really settle in any one place. That's one of the things I love about her.

•••••••••••

About a year after the funeral, I got a call from Curtis's mom. I was in the middle of my sentence: two years of supervised probation. She said she had something of his that I might want. She wouldn't tell me what it was over the phone. She came to see me. She sat in a hard kitchen chair and held her purse in her lap with both hands.

"I'm not sure where he got this thing. It's the oddest-looking thing." She unsnapped her purse and reached into it. "Do you know anything about it?" She held out the statue of Elvis Christ to me.

I took it from her hand. Some of the paint had chipped off. Elvis was missing the blue paint off one of his eyes. It looked like he was winking.

I gazed at the Elvis statue, unable to look away. I was sure I had left it on the dash in Elvis's Stutz Blackhawk. "We got that from a guy we saw get killed while we were out on the road. How did you get it?"

"It was returned with his personal items. They told me that when they found him, he was holding it in his hand."

"Yeah?" I asked.

She nodded.

It was at that moment that I was sure his death hadn't been an accident. I couldn't help but cry, and his mom cried too, even though she didn't understand why I had suddenly lost control like I had. I asked her if I could keep it. She nodded, then asked, "What does it mean?"

"Nothing." I rubbed my thumb against the smooth ivory. "Don't mean nothing."

I spent many hours in the dead dark of many nights lying in my bed, puzzling over how Curtis ended up with that statue. Maybe he came across one at some gift shop or store he stopped at after he left me. Or maybe I don't remember it right. Maybe I never took that statue with me. I just thought I did, but actually, I had left it in the Dart. But I was sure I had brought it with me that night. I was sure I had set it on the dash of Elvis's Stutz Blackhawk. I was certain. But maybe Curtis went back later that night, after the ambulance hauled me away. For whatever reason, he couldn't go on without it, or he went back to check on me, to try to find me, and came across it. But maybe. Just maybe it was something else. Something else entirely. Something that defies a reasonable explanation. Something that goes beyond what I can readily believe can happen in this world. I know what I would like to believe. But the only thing that I'm certain of is that it was there with Curtis in the end, and in the end, he's the only one who could tell you for sure.

•••••••••••

My sentence ended a week ago. The last I heard from Becky, she had gone north to Rhode Island. She wrote that her place was near the ocean and only a mile or so from a lighthouse. That was six months ago. I wonder if she's still there. Somehow I doubt it.

When I read over her letters, I always manage to think back to that night in Mississippi when we both slept wrapped tight in her sleeping bag. And if I close my eyes, I can almost smell her auburn hair. Like when I think of Curtis, I always see him driving that Dart of his with one scarred hand on the wheel and the other resting on the open window, the wind blasting his body.

It's hard for me to think of Curtis as dead. I guess because, in my mind, he isn't. He's still out there on the road somewhere. Driving. Trying to make it to Canada. Trying to make it anywhere he can find some peace. Sometimes, I expect him to pull up, and we'll go off to the places that we used to go: the airport, the beach, or just hit the interstate and take off. I know it will never happen.

And now that I have regained my freedom, the road calls to me. More and more, I have found myself wanting to make that trip north. I'm certain that I will one night.

One night, when the moon is high and bright and looks like it's been smudged by a heavy thumbprint. When a dry dust scratches the back of my throat like the longing for quiet in the midst of chaos. When a cool breeze tugs at my clothes and carries a vague scent of pine like the essence of all my hope. When the road is empty and a late night mist rises from the ground like a million lost souls, I will.

# Acknowledgments

I want to thank the following people, all of whom contributed greatly in various capacities.

Thanks to the fine teachers at Florida International University—Lynne Barrett, John Dufresne, and Les Standiford—for their valued lessons in the craft of fiction. I still consider myself (and always will consider myself) their student.

To my family for their support over the years I have worked on this novel.

To the Tampa Writers Alliance—although I never presented any portion of this story to the group for review, valued critiques I received on other pieces of writing were applied here.

To all the editors and contributors at Wise Ink for their help in taking this novel on the final leg of its journey.

To Alicia Dean for her contributions to an earlier draft.

And finally, to the people who lived through parts of this with me: Andy, Bruce, Jim, Kenny, Tony, and Steve.

# Biography

John Slayton is a graduate of the Master of Fine Arts program in creative writing at Florida International University. His fiction and poetry have appeared in numerous magazines and anthologies.

John works in the field of information technology and resides in Tampa, Florida. He likes to play tennis with his beautiful wife Sandra and his daughter Sara.